"THE FORCES OF EVIL"

Halloween is the time we confront the forces of evil, when devils, imps, witches, and goblins are on the prowl.

Halloween can inspire mystery stories in which the atmosphere of Halloween heightens the natural suspense already present; or fantasy stories that are rooted in the witches, goblins, and devils that are inseparable from the celebration; or horror stories that take advantage of the effluvium of evil that clings to the day.

In this anthology, you will find examples of all three.

—From the Introduction by Isaac Asimov

Other Avon Books edited by
Carol-Lynn Rössel Waugh,
Martin Harry Greenberg and Isaac Asimov

THE BIG APPLE MYSTERIES
SHOW BUSINESS IS MURDER
THE TWELVE CRIMES OF CHRISTMAS

13 HORRORS OF HALLOWEEN

EDITED BY
CAROL-LYNN RÖSSEL WAUGH,
MARTIN HARRY GREENBERG
AND ISAAC ASIMOV

 AVON
PUBLISHERS OF BARD, CAMELOT, DISCUS AND FLARE BOOKS

THIRTEEN HORRORS OF HALLOWEEN is an original publication of Avon Books. This work has never before appeared in book form.

Additional Copyright notices appear on the acknowledgments page and serve as an extension of this Copyright page.

AVON BOOKS
A division of
The Hearst Corporation
1790 Broadway
New York, New York 10019

First Avon Printing, October, 1983

AVON TRADEMARK REG. U. S. PAT. OFF. AND IN OTHER COUNTRIES, MARCA REGISTRADA, HECHO EN U. S. A.

Printed in the U. S. A.

WFH 10 9 8 7 6 5 4 3 2 1

ACKNOWLEDGMENTS

"Halloween," by Isaac Asimov. Copyright © 1975 by American Airlines. From *American Way Magazine*. Reprinted by permission of the author.

"Unholy Hybrid," by William Bankier. Copyright © 1963 by Mercury Press, Inc. From *The Magazine of Fantasy and Science Fiction*. Reprinted by permission of Curtis Brown, Ltd.

"Trick-or-Treat," by Anthony Boucher. Copyright © 1946 by Anthony Boucher. Reprinted by permission of Curtis Brown, Ltd.

"The October Game," by Ray Bradbury. Copyright © 1950; copyright renewed 1975 by Ray Bradbury. Reprinted by permission of the Harold Matson Company, Inc.

"Halloween Girl," by Robert Grant. Copyright © 1982 by TZ Publications, Inc. Reprinted by permission of the author.

"Day of the Vampire," by Edward D. Hoch. Copyright © 1972 by H. S. D. Publications, Inc. Reprinted by permission of the author.

"Night of the Goblin," by Talmage Powell. Copyright © 1981 by Talmage Powell. Reprinted by permission of the author and his agents, the Scott Meredith Literary Agency, Inc., 845 Third Ave., New York, NY 10022.

"The Adventure of the Dead Cat," by Ellery Queen. Copyright © 1946; copyright renewed 1952 by Ellery Queen. Reprinted by permission of the agent for the author's estate, the Scott Meredith Literary Agency, Inc., 845 Third Ave., New York, NY 10022.

"Pumpkin Head," by Al Sarrantonio. Copyright © 1982 by Al Sarrantonio. Reprinted by permission of the author.

For Reynald, Arlette and Fabien Pinard,
and Nadia Bacha, of France,
who had their introduction to
American life and its
"curious customs" one Halloween
in the State of Maine.

CONTENTS

Introduction: THE FORCES OF EVIL

by Isaac Asimov

Halloween is the time we confront the forces of evil, when devils, imps, witches, and goblins are on the prowl, and that seems odd if you stop to think about it.

November 1 is All Saints' Day. Each saint has a day of his own—the day of his martyrdom, or of some other salient event in his life—but on All Saints' Day, all the saints are celebrated. An older term is All Hallows' Day; both "Hallow" and "Saint" are derived from the notion of "holiness," of "sanctification," of "devotion to the service of God," the former from the Teutonic, the latter from Latin.

Among the ancient peoples (and among Jews even today), the day was supposed to start at sunset. Thus, Christmas, by ancient standards, would start at sunset on December 24. That is why we make a fuss about "Christmas Eve." It is not just the evening before Christmas; it was originally the first part of Christmas itself. The same is true for "New Year's Eve."

Similarly, All Hallows' Day should start, by the old tradition, at sunset on October 31. That evening would be All Hallows' Eve, or All Hallows' Even, if we use the older abbreviation. All Hallows' Even is easily abbreviated to "Hallow Even" and, further, to "Halloween."

But then, how did a day that is devoted to all the saints, to all that is holy, come to be celebrated as a day when all the forces of evil are abroad? In fact, where do the forces of evil come from?

The ancients always recognized that both good and evil were abroad in the world, but the mythological treatment of this varied from culture to culture. The Greeks, for instance, tended to think that the gods were basically good, but that they could be angered; and when angered, they could subject humanity to evil. Thus, Apollo, the most attractive of the Greek gods, was not

11

only the source of youth, male beauty, sunlight, poetry, and medicine—but also of disease and plagues. When he was angry, the twanging of his bow shot down men, women, and children by the thousands.

In the Norse myths, on the other hand, there was a clearer separation of good and evil. The gods (Odin, Thor, and the rest, who were basically good) faced the eternal enmity of the evil giants, and between them was an endless war, which was presumably mirrored in the presence of both good and evil in the world. Even within the ranks of the gods there was evil, for Loki, the cleverest of the gods, was more spiteful and malicious than any giant.

In this respect, however, it was the Persian mythology that was most influential in the development of Halloween. Surprised? Well...

Zarathustra (Zoroaster), about 580 B.C., systematized the Persian dualistic view of the universe. There was a principle of good, Ahura Mazda (or Ormuzd), and a principle of evil, Ahriman, which were viewed as virtually independent of each other and very nearly equal. The creation of the world, its development and history, were all but incidents in the unending celestial warfare between these two principles, each leading a separate army of innumerable spirits. So even was the contest that it was necessary for human beings to choose sides, for even their puny power might sway the victory to one side or the other. (Naturally, it was to be hoped that as many human beings as possible would choose the good.)

The Jews were part of the Persian Empire for two centuries, from 538 B.C. to 330 B.C., and in that time, certain Persian notions penetrated their thinking.

Before the Persians took over, the Jews had thought of God as all in all, as the author of evil as well as good. Thus in 2 Samuel 24:1 the Bible says, "the anger of the Lord was kindled against Israel, and he moved David against them to say, Go, number Israel and Judah." David's census was apparently a sin (the Bible doesn't say why) and as a result, God afflicted Israel with a severe plague. God was both bringing about the sin, and punishing it as well.

Once the Persians came in, however, the Jews, while

retaining the thought that God was supreme and could not be permanently defeated or thwarted, created a formidable adversary who could cause him at least temporary trouble. This Judaistic Ahriman was named "Satan" (a Hebrew word meaning "adversary").

In the First Book of Chronicles (21:1), a retelling of Israel's history by people writing during or after the Persian domination, the incident of the census is told as follows: "And Satan stood up against Israel, and provoked David to number Israel."

It is now Satan's fault, and not God's.

As in the case of the Persian mythology, God and Satan were each at the head of an army of innumerable spirits, and by Roman times the popular religion was full of such spirits. The New Testament has a number of tales of evil spirits being cast out of human beings.

During and after Roman times, Christianity—which began as a Jewish sect, and which borrowed Jewish thinking on the subject of God, Satan, and their respective armies of spirits—slowly converted first the Roman Empire and then the rest of Europe. In the process, they encountered pagan gods. The Christians could see these only as evil spirits who, led by Satan, were masquerading as gods and misleading the people who followed them.

In Celtic Europe, notably in the British Isles, November 1 was considered the beginning of the year. The harvest was safely in and the winter's food supply was assured so the people could relax and enjoy themselves. They thanked their gods who, it was assumed, swarmed over the world with equal happiness.

To the Christians, the Celts were invoking evil spirits, but it was difficult to argue against such a joyous holiday. The Christians therefore took it over and called it "All Saints' Day"—all the holy saints and not all the evil spirits.

However, some of the people did not forget the joyous rites of the old Celts and these have survived after fifteen hundred years or so in the tiny ritual of trick-or-treat and in the stories of witches and goblins (the Christian view of the Celtic deity).

Nor is October 31 the only Halloween. May 1 was also a joyous day in pagan Europe. The fields were verdant, the weather was warm, and the sun was bright. The long winter was forgotten. With joy, people celebrated the time with fun and games (sometimes sexual) and we still have dim memories of it in the form of the Maypole, and the "Queen of the May."

Again, the Christians saw this as a worship of evil demons. May 1 is St. Walpurgis's (or Walburga's) Day, she being a British saint, and the evening of April 30, is St. Walpurgis's Eve, or, in German, *Walpurgisnacht*. The German version of Halloween occurs then, with devils and witches meeting on the mountain peak of the Brocken (something that is one of the highlights in Walt Disney's *Fantasia*).

Halloween reflects itself in our literature in three ways: in mystery stories in which the atmosphere of Halloween heightens the natural suspense already present; or fantasy stories that are rooted in the witches, goblins, and devils that are inseparable from the celebration; or horror stories that take advantage of the effluvium of evil that clings to the day.

In this anthology, you will find examples of all three.

HALLOWEEN

by Isaac Asimov

*Isaac Asimov doesn't really need an introduction, but it
is worth noting that this prolific and wonderful writer
of science fiction and science fact is also a notable mystery writer. His science fiction/crime hybrids* The Caves
of Steel *(1954) and* The Naked Sun *(1957) helped es-
tablish this form of literature, and his "Black Widowers"
series has a wide and devoted following.*

When Haley got there at last in the dark hours of the
early morning of November 1, it was all but over. The
plutonium was gone; the thief lay crumpled in a heap
at the bottom of the stairs on the twenty-fifth floor of
the hotel. The medical examiner was bending over him,
but it was clear the thief would never say anything
more. The report Haley had received said that the thief
had said one word, "Halloween," and died.

Haley allowed no expression to cross his hard-lined,
fortyish face. Briefly, he studied Sanderson, the local
security man at the station. He had met him before but
had reached no opinion about him, one way or the other.
Sanderson looked now as though he were on the point
of weeping, his faded blue eyes glistening in the dim
light.

Haley motioned the man to one side and said, "Who
was the thief, Sanderson? That was not made clear."

"He worked at the station."

"That much I know. Was he a nuclear physicist? Was
he one of your specialists?"

"No. He was a clerical worker. He was not in re-
search."

"That's worse. How would a clerical worker have
access to the plutonium?"

Sanderson looked troubled and grew sulky. "That

15

was a mistake on our part. We took him so for granted that we didn't see him. Human error." He shook his head.

"And what was the motive?"

"Ideology," Sanderson said. "He got the job just to do this. We know because he left a note behind, couldn't resist crowing over us. He was one of those who feel that nuclear fission is deadly; that it will lead to the big-time theft of plutonium, to the making of home-made bombs, to nuclear terrorism and blackmail."

"I take it he was out to show it could be done?"

"Yes. He was going to publicize it and rouse public opinion."

"How dangerous is the plutonium he stole?" Haley asked.

"Not at all dangerous. It's a small amount. You could hold the case in your hand. It wasn't even meant for the fissioning core. We were doing other things with it. There's certainly not enough to build a bomb with, I assure you."

"Could there be possible danger to the individual holding it?"

"None if it's left in its case. If you took it out, there would be damage eventually to anyone coming in contact with it."

"I could see where public alarm would be justified," Haley said.

Sanderson frowned. "But it proves nothing. It was a mistake that will never happen again and in any case, the alarm system worked. We were after him at once. If he hadn't managed to get to this hotel, if we didn't fear alarming the people here..."

"Why didn't you inform the Bureau at once?"

"If we could have gotten him ourselves..." Sanderson mumbled.

"Then the whole thing could have been hidden, even from the Bureau. Mistakes and all."

"Well..."

"But you did inform us in the end. After he died. I take it, therefore, you don't have the plutonium?"

Sanderson's eyes drifted furtively away from Haley's steady glance. "No, we don't." Then defensively: "We couldn't operate too openly. There were thousands of people here and if the notion arose that there was trouble—if it were pinned to the station..."

"Then you would have lost and he would have won, even if you caught him and retrieved the plutonium. I understand that. How long was he here, then?" Haley looked at his watch. "It's 3:57 A.M. now."

"All day. It was only when it got late enough to allow us to work more openly that we trapped him on the stairs. We tried to rush him and he tried to run. He slipped—hit his head against the railing, after tumbling a flight, and fractured his skull."

"And he didn't have the plutonium on him. How do you know he had it with him when he entered the hotel?"

"It was seen. One of our men almost had him at one point."

"So during the hours he managed to evade you in this hotel, he could have hidden this thing, a small box, anywhere on the twenty-nine floors, in the ninety rooms on each floor—or in the corridors, offices, utility sections, basement, roof—and we have to have it back, don't we? We can't allow plutonium to float about the city, however small the amount. Is that right?"

"Yes," Sanderson said unhappily.

"One alternative is to take a hundred men and search the hotel—floor by floor, room by room, square inch by square inch—until we find it."

"We can't do that," Sanderson said. "How would we explain it?"

"And what is the alternative?" Haley asked. "Do we have a hint? The thief said something. 'Halloween'?"

Sanderson nodded. "He was conscious a few moments before he died. We asked him where the plutonium was and he said, 'Halloween.'"

Haley took a deep breath and let it out slowly. "Is that all he said?"

"That's all. Three of us heard him."

"And it was definitely 'Halloween' you heard? He didn't say 'hollow ring,' for instance?"

"No. 'Halloween.' We all agree."

"Has the word any significance to you? Is there a Project Halloween at the station? Is the word used to mean something in an in-way?"

"No, no. Nothing like that."

"Do you think he was trying to tell you where the plutonium was?"

"We don't *know*," said Sanderson agonizingly. "His eyes were unfocused. It was a dying whisper. We don't even know if he heard our question."

Haley was silent for a moment. "Yes. It could have been a last fugitive thought of anything at all. A childhood memory. Anything—except that yesterday was Halloween. The day on which he hid in this hotel and tried to evade you for long enough to get the story to the newspapers was Halloween. It could have had some significance to him."

Sanderson shrugged.

Haley was thinking out loud. "Halloween is the day on which the forces of evil are abroad and he must surely have been considering himself to be fighting those forces."

"We are not evil," Sanderson said.

"What counts is what *he* thought—and he didn't want himself caught, and the plutonium, too. So he hid it. Every room is vacuumed, every room has its sheets and towels changed at some time during the day, and when that is happening the door is open. He could pass an open door and step in—one step and a quick placing of the box where it wouldn't be readily seen. Then he could come back later to retrieve it; or if he was caught, the box would eventually be noticed by some guest or some employee, taken to the management, and recognized with or without having done damage."

"But *what* room?" Sanderson agonized.

"We can try *one* room," Haley said, "and if that doesn't work, we will have to search the hotel." He left.

Haley was back in half an hour. The body had been removed, but Sanderson was still there, deep in dejection.

"There were two people in the room," Haley said. "We had to wake them. I found something on top of the shelf above the coatrack. Is this it?"

It was a small cube, gray in color, heavy in the hand, the top held down by wing nuts.

"That's it," Sanderson said with barely controlled excitement. He loosened the wing nuts, lifted the top a crack, and put a small probe near the opening. The sound of crackling could be heard at once. "That's it. But how did you know where it was?"

"Just a chance," said Haley with a shrug. "The thief had Halloween on his mind, judging from his last word. When he saw a particular hotel room open and being cleaned, perhaps it seemed like an omen to him."

"What hotel room?"

"Room 1031," Haley said. "October the thirty-first. Halloween."

UNHOLY HYBRID

by William Bankier

William Bankier was born in Belleville, Ontario, Canada, and began writing when he was ten years old. His first published story, in Liberty *Magazine (Toronto) won a Canadian Short Story of the Month Prize. With his family, he moved to London in 1974, leaving behind a job as creative director of a Montreal advertising agency. He writes full-time, when he is not involved with amateur theatrics, music, or spectator sports. In 1980, along with Clark Howard, Ed Hoch, and John Lutz, he was nominated for an Edgar for best mystery short story.*

With soil like this, Sutter Clay said to himself, it's a wonder the stones don't put down roots and grow. Pressing his long, white fingers into the ground, he scooped up a double handful of damp earth and let it fall in clods and crumbles back into the black furrow.

Why, if I let my hands stay in this soil long enough, Clay continued his thoughts, they'd take root themselves. A thin smile bent the corner of Sutter Clay's pale mouth as he imagined his fingers thrust deep into the nourishing ground while a shiny filigree of roots crept from beneath his fingernails in search of food and moisture.

Good soil had been a factor in Sutter Clay's success as a gardener. No question about that. But there was more of Clay himself in the things he grew than there was of luck or nature, and if thumbs ever really were green, this thin young man would have had one of emerald and one of jade.

The few people who knew Sutter Clay, for he was a lonely man living out here on the edge of town, claimed he could grow oak trees in the Sahara Desert. At the County Exhibition every autumn, when folks trekked out to the Fair Grounds for the harness racing and the midway, those who knew what real wonders were would head for the produce pavilion to see what Sutter Clay had brought in this year. And Clay never disappointed them.

There, spread out in extravagant display as from a cornucopia, lay all the ripeness and abundance, all the browns and greens and reds and yellows of harvest home. Pumpkins the size of carriage wheels lay beneath the table lest they split the sturdy trestles that supported the rough planking. Eggplants, almost obscene in their bursting purple opulence; squash in a riot of bizarre shapes and textures; golden ears of corn with the husk shucked back in an immodest exposition of giant kernels straining for a hold on cobs scarcely big enough to hold so many; and even the humble turnip, inflated to the size of a football and ringed about like Saturn with alternate shades of mauve and ivory.

And the hybrids! Clay placed these on a separate table, each strange item carefully labeled with its name and details of its odd ancestry. Here was a cluster of crab apples with translucent skins, clinging to one stem like emperor grapes. Beside them, a bunch of carrots...carrots in name, shape, and size, but tinted the deep purple of beets. And ranged in rows were ears of spectacular corn spotted with multicolored kernels, some sparse as dominoes, some speckled like terrazzo floors, a mosaic of rainbow corn.

And behind it all, jealously watching lest someone touch part of the display, hovered the gaunt form of Sutter Clay, his long wrists dangling inches out of the sleeves of his shiny blue suit, his pale hair spread long and fine across the dome of his head, looking like nothing else so much as a swatch of silk from one of his precious ears of corn.

Yes, Sutter Clay could make things grow. He could make them grow bigger, and different than they had ever grown before. But there was no denying this deep, sweet-smelling black loam had a lot to do with it. As Clay crumbled a clod, a fat dew worm, belted and banded with rings of copper, humped and glistened between his fingers. He let the cold, pulsing worm slip gently to the ground and watched it thread its way into the soil.

"Go, my little cultivator," he said aloud. And as he spoke, a chilly April breeze fanned across the field and touched him through his scanty shirt. The spring afternoon was falling away into the woods behind the house and the pale blue silence of day's end was hanging in the sky.

Sutter Clay stood up and took his hoe and trowel and fork in one hand and his jacket in the other and headed for the house. There was smoke rising from the chimney. He wondered what Bonina would have for him tonight.

She was a girl who had come alone down the highway one night in January when snow whipped sideways past Sutter Clay's kitchen window. The car whose hospitality she had accepted turned off on the Brightsville Road and let her out a hundred yards from the small blue and white farmhouse. On such a night she could barely make it to Sutter's door. Nobody could ask her to go farther.

Bonina Ames was from a city up north. She had no family left, and having heard tell of friends in Lauderdale, she had set out down through the mountains to try to find them. Unless something worthwhile happened along the way. She smiled at Sutter with watery round eyes when she said this and would tell him no more. So he never did find out any more about Bonina Ames or where she came from.

But he knew as he looked at her that she was one of the homeliest women he had ever seen. Her head was the shape of a gourd; small at the top where not much hair at all struggled to cover a thin, bony forehead, then bloating and distending downward to an inflated jaw with puffed cheeks and a wide mouth that rippled when she talked and collapsed into a fat pout when she was silent. Her eyes were pale green and constantly wet like sliced grapes. She had, Clay noticed when she stood up, a tolerable body, poorly managed.

Well, there was nothing else for it but to have her stay the night. Then the storm stayed for another day and a night and so did Bonina Ames. By this time, she was making meals and knew where the dishpan was. When the weather cleared, Sutter never got around to asking her to leave and she showed no signs of gath-

ering her meagre belongings together in the shopping
bag which was all she had carried when she arrived.
So she stayed, doing a good job of cooking and cleaning,
and sleeping in the spare room on a cot that Clay knocked
together with some two-by-fours and a spring of chicken
wire.

And this was where Sutter Clay found Bonina when
he entered the house on that cool April evening. There
was a fire in the stove and the kitchen was warm. But
there was no pot in sight, nor any sign of activity around
the counter top. A sob from the bedroom caught Clay's
ear. He went in and stood over her.

"Are you sick?" he asked.

"Not actually."

"Then, what's the matter? Where's supper?"

"I just couldn't keep my mind on it. I'm so worried."

"Then something is wrong. What is it?"

She turned over and exposed the bloated face, glistening with tears. Her nose was running.

"Blow your nose," Sutter said.

"Oh, Sutter, I'm worried to death. I was hoping all
along something would happen. But nothing has. I'm
sure I'm pregnant."

Clay put his hands together and cracked his knuckles,
sucking in his pale lower lip. "It was the end of January,
wasn't it?" he said.

"Yes."

"Then, why didn't you say something sooner? Three
months. Pretty hard to do anything about it now."

"I know." She sat up and put her head in her hands.
"What are we going to do?"

Sutter Clay looked at her for a moment. Then he
said, "Don't you worry, everything's going to be all
right."

Into her hands, Bonina said, "How can it be, unless
we get married?" But Sutter did not hear her. He was
on his way out to the porch. Here, he ran his fingers
over the shining handles of the implements, selecting,
finally, the spade. Then he went back inside.

He found Bonina Ames unmoved, sitting on the edge
of the cot, her head in her hands, bowed almost to the
level of her knees. Without a word, Clay swung the
spade above his head and brought the sharp edge of it

down on her extended neck with all the force he could muster. The blow almost decapitated her. She hung poised, her buttocks raised a few inches from the mattress, for a full second. Then she toppled forward against the wall of the room and sank to the floor.

It became a busy night for Sutter Clay. First he went down to the far cornfield and used the same spade to dig a pit in the soft, rich earth. It was easy digging, which was just as well since he had to work in darkness. Then he returned to the house, gathered Bonina's belongings and put them in a bundle with the body and carried all together down to the grave. When she was covered over, he spread the excess earth about and broke the ground in the area into a series of furrows. Tomorrow he would plant and that would be the end of it. He would make a point of telling them at the store that his domestic had packed and lit out as suddenly as she had come. Must have been waiting out the winter. No family. No friends who knew her whereabouts. No questions. Let it lie.

And it all happened just as Sutter Clay had planned it. No questions were asked. No inquiries were made. And the warm summer days came and cast their sunlight and rain on all the fertile seeds Clay had planted in the earth. In the farthest field the corn grew tall, taller than ever, Sutter told himself with a grim smile. Then, with his natural sense of land economy, he planted pumpkins at the foot of the cornstalks.

Thus August followed July, and there was no drought this year. Sutter Clay smiled up into the friendly sky and the sun smiled back and gave way to just the right amount of rain at the proper time. Then September followed August and impressed its long, ripening days on the fields, which were now becoming heavy with the fruits of the land. Clay busied himself with final cultivation before harvest time but there was little for him to do now. He had done his work. The good earth was now doing her share.

When October arrived, it became obvious that this was a bumper year, even for a Sutter Clay. Day by day now, with admirable efficiency, Sutter began bringing in the produce.

"All things bright and beautiful, All creatures great

and small," he sang as he bent to the baskets and trundled wagonload after wagonload to root cellar and kitchen.

It was late October, Halloween was only a few days away, when Sutter worked his way to the farthest field. The corn was superb and he harvested it quickly, selecting superior ears for showing at the Exhibition.

And it was then that he saw the pumpkin. It was not a large pumpkin, about the size of a human head, resting on the black earth over the spot where Bonina Ames was buried. It was the obscene shape of the orange vegetable that stopped Clay rigid in his tracks. The thing was gourd-shaped; small at the top, then bloating out at the base like a gross, misshapen jaw. Above this, two inflated areas puffed out like cheeks and atop the whole unsightly growth there rested a swatch of pale corn silk that hung down in a shiny fringe around the gnarled dome.

Clay could not believe his eyes. Was the stuff actually growing there as it appeared to be? Or had it fallen from an ear of corn during the harvest, assuming this bizarre position to mock him? Sutter knelt down and grasped the silky substance. Then he drew back his hand in horror. The stuff felt more like hair than corn silk, and it seemed warm between his fingers. What hellish hybrid was this?

Later that night, Clay told himself that the stuff was warm only from the rays of the sun. As for the fact that it was growing on a pumpkin—well, anything can happen in a garden. He had proved it many times himself. Some sort of accidental cross-pollination. There was the explanation. Naturally, his imagination had been ready to play tricks on him once he found himself in the far field. He would just go down there tomorrow and root the thing out.

But Sutter Clay did not go into the farthest field on the morrow. Instead, he busied himself cleaning up off bits of harvesting on other parts of the farm. Then he went into town the next day and let it be known that he had a surfeit of pumpkins on his land, which were free for the taking.

The response was spectacular. By the carload the people came, anxious to pick up a pumpkin or two, what with Halloween only a day away and all. Sutter Clay locked himself in his house while the people were on his land and didn't stir till he had heard the last car depart.

When he did step outside, he almost fell over the pumpkin on the porch. Its ugly head was tipped backward so that it stared full up at him over bloated cheeks, and the fringe of yellow hair glistened palely in the vanishing rays of the sun. There was a note slipped under one side of the protruding jaw. Sutter bent down and fished it out, feeling a chill of revulsion as his hand brushed the skin of the thing.

"Mr. Clay," the note read, "this one appears to be some sort of a mixture. We thought you would want to keep it for the Exhibition."

Clay crumpled the note and dropped it to the ground. His first impulse was to kick the thing as far down the lane as his boot would send it. But for some reason, the impulse died. Instead of kicking, he bent down and picked up the pumpkin and carried it into the kitchen. It was surprisingly heavy for only a medium-sized vegetable. He set it on the kitchen table and went to find the whiskey.

With the bottle of bourbon on his lap and a glass in his hand, Sutter Clay sat near the window in the dusk and stared at the pumpkin on the table. As he drank, the room darkened and with each new wash of gray that overlapped the scene, the malevolent creature on the table took on a new dimension. Where there had been only fat cheeks, now there were tiny eyes; the jutting jaw now had pouting lips; and the whole evil head seemed to shift and frown and cast all manner of rueful glances at Sutter Clay.

By midnight the bottle was empty and Clay had fallen into a fitful sleep. Suddenly he woke up with a start. Was the table closer to him, or was it a trick of the darkness? The murk was now pierced only by a shaft of milky moonlight.

Clay looked at his watch: 12:15. So, it was now the thirty-first of October. All Hallows' Eve. A day for torment and wickedness, if ever there was one. Sutter Clay stood up and took three unsteady steps toward the table. The last brought his thigh up heavily against it and set the table rocking on its legs. The pumpkin lurched and moved an inch closer to Clay. He grunted with fear and rage and struck out at it with his fist. Was it more imagination or did the thing feel soft and yielding under his knuckles? It was fresh from the field. It should be crisply solid.

Suddenly Sutter Clay knew what he was going to do. Stumbling to the cabinet by the sink, he fumbled about and found matches and a candle. Striking a light, he dropped hot wax in a saucer and stuck the candle upright. Then he opened a drawer and selected a sharp knife.

Returning to the table, he set the candle down beside the pumpkin and pulled his chair over with one foot. He sat down. Oh, what winking, grimacing faces the thing made now, contorting its bloated features under the dancing light of the candle.

"So it's a face you want?" Sutter Clay said aloud. "Then, we'll give you the one you deserve!" And with that, he plunged the knife full depth into the pumpkin shell.

As he drew the knife out, there was a hissing sound, almost as though a child had sighed, and the room was suddenly full of the fetid odor of the grave. Clay, however, was beyond terror now. Snorting his nostrils clear of the foul, musty gas, he made further incisions in the husk of the pumpkin until he had cut the top off in a clean circle.

Lifting the section off by the hair, he began scooping out the pulp, letting the cold, stringy slime fall writhing onto his trousers and down the legs of the chair. When all was scooped out, he punctured gross, triangular eyes, a small round nose, and a wide, grinning mouth with one pointed tooth hanging down in the traditional Halloween fashion. No jack-o'-lantern had ever looked so evil.

"Now, let your light so shine before men," Sutter Clay said as his brain spewed thoughts from a church service of long ago, "that they may see your good works." With that, he took the candle from the saucer, poured hot wax into the hollow skull and set the candle inside. With the fringed cap replaced, the job was done.

Clay pushed his chair back a foot or so and inspected

his work. The jack-o'-lantern guttered and winked and a liquid hiss escaped its leering mouth. Clay slapped his knees and laughed hysterically. The force of the laugh burst against the pumpkin and caused the flame to dance wildly inside the crackling head.

Then Sutter Clay fell silent. For as he watched, the mouth of the creature, which had been a mischievous grin, sagged at the corners and collapsed into a grievous pout. And two drops of wax appeared at the corners of the triangular eyes and trickled slowly down the golden cheeks.

Clay's lips were dry. He licked them with a tongue that was no longer moist. Then, as he watched trans-fixed, a tiny tongue of fire darted from the corner of the drooping mouth and ran swiftly across the table. Clay could only watch as the liquid fire dripped in a sparkling cascade from the edge of the table and splashed in a pool of sparks on the floor. Fed from above, the pool grew. Then it overflowed and moved across the floor toward the toe of Clay's boot.

Fascinated, Sutter Clay watched as the fire gushed from the livid mouth. He could smell leather burning, but he could not move. Then, as the flames caught hold and surrounded the chair, father and son sat in the burning kitchen and watched each other die.

Down in the town somebody looked at the northern sky and said, "Looks like Sutter Clay's place is on fire." So they called out the fire engine but it got there too late to save anything.

Raking the cold ruins next day, a fireman found the charred husk of the jack-o'-lantern with its stump of candle.

"Must have been some crazy Halloween prank," he muttered. "What kind of children are we raising these days, anyway?"

TRICK-OR-TREAT

by Anthony Boucher

*"Anthony Boucher" was a pen name used by the mystery
and science fiction writer William Anthony Parker White
(1911–1968). He was a founding co-editor of The Magazine of Fantasy and Science Fiction, that field's premier
quality publication, and wrote criticism of the genre under the name of "H. H. Holmes." He has at least eight
mystery novels to his credit, in addition to his short
stories, which have only recently been collected in* Ex-
eunt Murderers: The Best Mystery Stories of Anthony
Boucher *(Southern Illinois University Press, 1983).*

The radio said, "So remember, folks: murder, though it
has no tongue, will speak." A deep voice on a filter mike
echoed it horribly: *"Murder—will—speak!"* Then the
electric organ music came up loud.

Ben Flaxner clicked the switch. He said, "That's a
cheerful thought," and the outside corner of his left eye
began to twitch again.

Rose looked up from mending her pink housecoat. "I
don't see why you've got to keep listening to stuff like
that. As if it wasn't bad enough to be living in this
dump with your nerves all shot and—"

She broke off and gasped, "Oh!" as a terribly twisted
face goggled leeringly at the glass in the window. The
doorbell rang and Ben jumped. Then he saw the face
and grinned. "Kids," he said.

He answered the door and a high voice outside on
the sidewalk said, "Trick or treat!"

Ben laughed. "You kids got you a good racket. A
shakedown, we used to call it back in—" He glanced
back at Rose and stopped the sentence.

"Trick or treat!" the voice repeated.

"Treat," Ben said. He went across to the kitchen,

which was a part of the same room as the living room, and the bedroom too, for that matter. He came back with a double handful of hard candy.

Ben grinned as he shut the door. "Sometime I'll have to hold out on 'em," he said. "I'd like to see what they do for a trick. Usually they soap the windows, and with ours all soaped up already—"

"That's it," Rose snapped. "Remind me!" In repose her features were pretty, especially if she remembered all her makeup. Now they looked sharp and tight and a lot older. "Remind me I've got to live here in one little room with you *and* your brother, and it isn't even a room. A store, facing right on the street, where you've got to soap the windows so the customers won't look in and think you're an ad for tomato juice!"

Ben spoke a little slower even than usual. "Look, baby! Where's there a safer place to hole up? Berkeley's full of transients now—defense workers, service families. Nobody keeps an eye on strangers; there's too many of 'em. With Joe already working here, it was a natural."

"For how long?" Rose flared up.

Ben said, "So long as the heat is on."

"The cops couldn't pin it on you," she said.

Ben waved a big fist vaguely. "Yeah, but—"

The doorbell rang again. Ben's body jerked and his hand moved toward his hip. Then he relaxed, seeing another masked face.

He opened the door and heard "Trick or treat!" and went through all the routine again. When it was over, he fetched out a fifth and showed it to Rose. She shook her head and sat sullen. He poured himself a slug and held it up and said, "Here's to Halloween." He downed it and gasped. "I got to make some good contacts out here. This stuff....Rrrrr!"

"You won't make contacts sitting in here all day scared of your shadow."

He didn't hear her. "But damned if I don't like Halloween. I remember when Joe and me was kids. We used to have us a time, all right. And sometimes I think maybe that's what got me started—trick or treat. You walk up to some dope and you tell him '...or else!' It's all the same...Come on, honey, just one snort? For Halloween?"

"You couldn't get me something hot on that radio, could you? Or does it just play murders?"

The doorbell rang again, and Ben grinned happily at the little sheeted, masked figure outside. Rose groaned, and got up and fiddled with the dial herself. She heard Ben open the door and she heard the little voice say, "Trick or treat!" Then she heard the shots. When she turned, all she could see was a wisp of white sheet whisking away in the darkness, and Ben squatting there on the floor, holding his stomach with both hands.

He started to roll over backward as she reached him. Somehow it seemed very important to hold him up. Men aren't dead till they're stretched out. His lips were making noises, but there was a choking rattle in his throat that kept the lip noises from being words. Rose knelt there beside him, propping him up, and the tear she'd just mended ripped open again with the tension on her housecoat where she was kneeling on it, but with all that blood you could never clean it, anyway.

She thought silly thoughts like that because you can't think: He's dying here in my arms and the last words I said to him were mean. Then there weren't any more lip noises and she let go. But the body didn't just keel over backward. She'd been holding it somehow off balance and it started to topple toward her. She screamed one short, sharp, high scream and pushed at it. This time it did go over backward. She screamed again, and then after a while it seemed that screaming was all she could do—ever.

A key clicked, the door opened, and Joe was standing there. He slapped her face and said, "What do you want to do? Bring the whole street in here? What's Ben been—"

Then he saw the body and stopped. His next movements were quick and efficient. He shut the door behind him, making sure the latch caught. He went to the kitchen part of the room and brought her water. Then he fetched the fifth from the table. After a minute he said, "All right?"

She nodded and gulped. "All right."

Joe said bluntly, "Did you—?"

She choked. She tried to tell him, even if it didn't make any sense. "It was one of those kids, I thought. You know: 'Trick or treat!' And then it shot—"

Joe looked her over carefully. "All right," he said at last. "I'm not asking any questions. I don't know what it was Ben got mixed up in back in Chicago, and I don't want to know. I do know he was hiding out here and scared of his skin, and now something got him. It's tough but we've got to keep our noses clean."

Rose said, "You're strong, Joe. You've got sense, not like—"

"Whose gun is that?"

Rose hadn't seen the gun before. She shook her head. Joe said, "I'll get rid of it."

She nodded dumbly.

Joe thought aloud, sharply, decisively. "Nobody's showed up, so I guess they didn't hear you screaming. Lucky the stores on either side of us are still stores, and dark at night. You give me five minutes, then go up to the drugstore and call the police from there. Understand?"

Rose nodded again. Joe went close to her and put his hand on her soft upper arm. She pulled away. "We can't, Joe! Not with Ben—"

He shrugged his shoulders and walked out of the store.

She looked at her watch and took a drink. She tried not to look at what was on the floor. She sat there looking at the watch. Then the doorbell rang and a shrill voice said, "Trick or treat!"

When Joe came back, she was lying on the floor. She came to when he shook her, muttering, "It came back. It came back, Joe!"

"Huh? Oh, another trick or treat?"

"Joe, don't be so hard. How can you stand there—"

He gripped her by both shoulders. "Rose," he said, "I gave my brother a hideout. That's one thing. From now on I'm rid of him. I'm looking out for me—and you. Understand?" He went on rapidly. "The gun was easy. I got a San Francisco train, paid a local fare, rode to the next stop, and walked back. I left the gun there. It may turn up in San Francisco. Much more likely, some

Halloween drunk'll pick it up and we'll never hear of it again. We're rid of it—too," he added. "Now, get on that phone."

This is where I came in. You always come in late when you're on Homicide, so sometimes when you tell the story it's better to start in earlier and give out with a lot of stuff we didn't learn for a long time. That way, when you're reading it, you can get a picture a lot quicker than I did when I walked into that store.

There isn't anything uncommon about people living in stores in Berkeley. You walk down Telegraph and that's what you see every place. Little one-man stores closed up because the President sends greetings, and meanwhile all the defense workers pile into town and there's no place to sleep. Sure, it was tough—a man and his wife and his brother all living in a one-room store, but at least they didn't have any kids.

I've been in some of the stores—professionally and otherwise—and they've looked real nice. Trim and neat and damned near like home. I walked into this one, and the first thing I thought was how glad I was I wasn't married to this woman. Squalor's the word, I guess. Everybody's junk everyplace.

The people's name was Flaxner and she was the corpse's wife and this was her brother-in-law. She was average height and pretty in a thin, sharp way. The brother-in-law looked like Humphrey Bogart or was going to die trying. He worked in a plant out at Richmond. The dead husband was unemployed, which was a word I haven't written down on a form in years. Well, he was unemployed now, all right.

I went over the story with each of them alone and both of them together, and it still made just as much or as little sense. They didn't either of them seem afraid of the police. They answered questions clearly and readily, but not too clearly and readily. I don't know what made me think they were covering something.

Rose Flaxner timed the shot about seven-forty because the radio chiller they'd been listening to was over at seven-thirty. I asked Joe Flaxner where he was then.

"I was at a movie—Halloween horror bill up at the Campus Theatre. Don't go."

"Thanks," I said. "Times?"

"Let's see—I get in from Richmond in the car pool about four-thirty. The show probably runs about four hours, but I couldn't stick it all. I walked out around seven-thirty. That's a quarter of an hour from here by foot."

The doctor said seven-forty was as likely as anything. All the time I was getting the story he was busy, and so was the fingerprint man (feeling kind of annoyed because there really wasn't anything to print but the corpse), and the boys were covering the block hunting for a gun or anything else.

They didn't find the gun, but they found something else. Down at the corner, stuffed into a trash can, Rourke found a sheet and a mask. I showed them to Rose.

She shuddered. She wouldn't ever think masks were funny again. She said, "I wouldn't know. They all look alike. But it could be the same. I don't know."

I asked the usual one about has your husband got any enemies.

To hear them talk, there wasn't ever anybody alive that had so few enemies as the late Ben Flaxner. I looked at his ugly puss and I looked at Rose and I didn't believe it. But all I said was, "All right. Everybody loved him and I don't doubt they're taking up funds for a Flaxner memorial right now. But somebody killed him. All right. Who'd you know five feet or under?"

They looked at me and I got patient like George Burns trying to explain something. I said, "This is maybe the smartest killer I've ever run up against. He picks the one night in the year when he can go around completely disguised without bothering anybody. Then he ditches the sheet and the mask and there's not a thing to tie him to the crime. But to bring it off, he'd have to be little. You saw the tick-or-treater; so did your husband. Both of you would've thought there was something screwy if it hadn't looked like a kid. So who's under five feet? The killer has to be."

I was watching Rose, and something scared her and scared her bad. But I could see from the way she compressed her lips that I wasn't going to be able to find out what, just by asking. So I let it slide for the moment.

Then, suddenly, Joe exclaimed, "The hunchback!"

Rose looked suddenly relieved and she said, "The hunchback!" too.

"Of course," Joe went on. "I don't know who he is, but I've seen him around this neighborhood a lot. And one day when I came home he was having some kind of row with Ben. I don't know what. Ben wouldn't talk. But he's—oh, hell, he isn't over four eight, I'd say."

I wrote it down and waited. Finally Rose said, "He-len?"

Joe said, "Hell no. Why?"

I asked, "Who?"

"Helen Kirk," Rose said. "She's a friend of ours, works out where Joe does. She didn't hardly know Ben, but she *is* little—not over five feet. You know—the cute type."

I wrote down the name and the address she gave me and drew a cat in the margin, which was nice for Halloween.

"We're not on the same shift," Joe said. "She's on swing—she'll be getting home about twelve-thirty or one. So of course she was working when—"

I said, "Of course."

There wasn't much more to say right then. I finally said to Joe, "Richmond's in the next county. That's out of my territory. If it won't hold up national armament too much, I'd just as soon you stuck around here tomorrow. I'll want to see you again."

Joe said, "Can do, I guess."

The next hour or two was a lot of routine. There were forms to fill out and then waiting while they dug out the bullets. There were three of them, all from the same .32. I put the ballistics description and the corpse's prints on the wires to Washington, where the big file is, and to Cheyenne, where Rose Flaxner said they'd come from, and to Chicago, because she'd said "Ch—Cheyenne" and that was the likeliest name for her to've almost let slip.

When I got through, it was about time for Helen Kirk to be getting off work. She was a rare lucky woman in Berkeley. She had an apartment—on Alcatraz, not too far from the Flaxner's shop. I got into the apartment house without troubling anybody and camped in front of her door.

She showed up at two-thirty and there was a Marine

with her. They'd been bowling. The Marine looked as if he'd like to use me to knock down a few pins, but my badge calmed him down a little. He went away and Helen let me into the apartment.

She was little—four eleven, I'd guess—and just plump enough. She wasn't too cute, either. Just sort of lively. She liked an adventure like a policeman at two in the morning, but she didn't like it when I told her about Ben Flaxner. She took it harder than the people who knew him better, and maybe that proved something about Ben.

"It was Joe you mostly knew in the Flaxner family?" I asked.

"Yes. I used to see a lot of him." She stopped and then added, "Before Rose came out here." She didn't say anything more, just let it sink in unornamented.

I said, "That's a break for the Marines."

She asked, "But why did you come to see me, Lieutenant? I told you I scarcely knew Ben. He was grumpy and nervous and afraid; you couldn't know him."

"Afraid?"

"Like a child sometimes, that thinks something's going to get him. He was—oh, I don't know—funny."

I turned that around in my mind. I asked, "You clock in on time tonight?"

She said, "I guess so. I've never been docked yet."

I thought of a lot of swell possibilities on the way home. Maybe there was some way of faking a time clock at the Richmond plant. Sure it was possible, but it took a lot of believing. Those plants aren't run for fun.

Or maybe there never was a trick or treat. Joe and Rose made up the whole story between them, and there wasn't anybody under five feet. But would they make up such a wild story and carry it out so far as to plant a mask and a sheet?

Well, there was still the hunchback. If there was a hunchback. And in the meantime I could use some sleep.

The phone woke me up. It was Rose Flaxner. I guess they gave her my number at headquarters. She sounded half-crazy. She kept saying he was gone and she was all alone and it would come back and she was scared of what sounded like an angel; I didn't know for sure.

I boiled it down to where Joe hadn't been able to get off at Richmond and had gone on out there.

I said, "I'll talk to the plant manager and send a man out there to bring him back. Keep quiet about it, because it isn't strictly legal, but I think it'll work." I didn't tell her she was safe enough, anyway, because there was a man watching the storefront.

"Thank God!" she said in a kind of gasp. "Because it might come back."

"Lady, Halloween's over. This is November first."

"Yes—but you said it had to be little, and the—" She stopped short, then added, "I want to get out of this place. I'm afraid." Then suddenly she hung up.

You can't get anywhere on a phone anyway. I brushed my teeth, shaved and fixed breakfast and wondered what it was like to be a private eye like you read about, and have whiskey instead of coffee. I didn't think it'd work, but you never know till you try.

They had reading matter for me at headquarters. There wasn't anything yet from Cheyenne, not that I expected it, but there was plenty from Washington and Chicago. It started out like routine and it ended with cold fingers on my spine.

They knew Ben Flaxner's prints both places. That was his real name, and maybe it's smart to use your real name sometimes. Back before Repeal, they knew him very well in Chicago. Nothing big—just a young punk getting his start. He didn't do so good for a while after that; the depression hit all kinds of business. He got really going again with the war, and in the meantime he'd grown up.

He was 4-F and there was some suspicion of fraud, but his draft board had never been able to get hold of him for a re-physical. He got into the black market in Chicago—mostly liquor, which was a racket he knew backwards. He was doing swell until Johnny Angelino got his. The Chicago cops never pinned anything on him, but Johnny's friends had their own ideas. I began to see why he was out here and why he was jumpy and scared the way Helen Kirk said. It looked clear enough until you read the ballistics report.

It said that the type and make of the gun that had killed Flaxner was not too common and that the same sort of gun had been used on Johnny Angelino. They'd like to take a look at the slug in a comparison.

I didn't like the implications in that. But what really started the ice-fingers playing with my vertebrae was this:

Johnny Angelino—the Angel, they called him, not just from his name but from that round sweet face with the curls—was a dwarf.

Four feet one, it said. Just the right size for a trick-or-treat.

Ghosts don't come back and kill their murderers with the same gun. I know better than that. So do you. So did Ben Flaxner.

I didn't pay any attention to it. I didn't give it another thought. But if Berkeley had bars, which it doesn't, I might have tried the methods of a private eye before I started out hunting for the hunchback.

Joe Flaxner said he'd seen the hunchback around the neighborhood a lot, so I tried the neighborhood stores—the ones that were still really being stores. The drugstore never saw him, neither did the service station man. The barber saw him a couple of times—he remembered because he thought it brought him luck with the gee-gees—but he didn't know anything.

Then I tried the butcher. He was all alone with some brains and tripe and his memories. He said, "Hunchback? Well, he *has* been in here."

"Lately?" I asked.

"Not for a week or so."

He looked like he wanted to talk and still he didn't. I tried showing my badge and it worked. He said, "So you got him, huh?"

I deadpanned it with a grunt.

He said, "You see how it is, officer. I want to see him get it, but I don't want to start anything, see? I don't want any trouble."

"I understand."

"That foreigner up the street, now; I bet he took some of them hens. Made a nice profit on 'em, too, I'll bet you. But I don't want to go breaking ceilings. I don't want any trouble."

"Sure," I said. "There's a war on."

"That's it, officer. That's exactly it. So I told him to

take his black market chickens and—well, I sure told him. But I didn't want to go to the OPA about it and report it because—"

"—you don't want any trouble."

"That's it."

"Supposing you changed your mind?"

"Huh?"

"Supposing you wanted some hens, after all. He leave any instructions?"

It took five minutes after that. I timed it by the wall clock. He kept going back and forth between "there was a war on" and he "didn't want any trouble." Finally he dug out the card from under the cash register and I thanked him and told him I'd be in as a customer next time I wanted some tripe, and I hope I live that long.

The address was over in West Berkeley, across the railroad tracks. It was in the basement of an old house made into flats. I knocked on the door the way it said on the card and he opened up, and sure enough he was a hunchback and only about four nine.

He had a long face with a Roman beak and his voice was Italian. He asked, "What you want?" and I said, "In, first of all."

He backed away and let me in. His room made the Flaxner store look elegant, but it was cleaner. He sat down by the grappa bottle, but I kept standing near the door.

He said, "What you want?" again.

I said, "Talk. We can do it here if you like. If you don't, they've got rooms as nice as this down on McKinley Avenue."

He snarled a word in Italian that maybe meant copper, only I think it went a little deeper than that. He made a move with his right hand, and I had my .45 in mine.

I said, "You're handling black-market poultry. That's none of my business. My business is corpses. And you had a row with a corpse of mine, and it just so happens he used to play black-market games, too. It takes some clearing up."

He wasn't talking. He hunched himself over a little more than nature had done and sat there. I smelled second-hand garlic and olive oil. He leaned forward a little and spat at my feet. I didn't care. It was his carpet.

I said, "All right. You won't talk to me, you'll talk to the boys."

He said, "Will I?" and just then I felt the rod in my spine.

I hadn't heard the newcomer make his entrance; he was good. I didn't argue when he said, "Drop." I let the .45 go; I slipped the safety catch back on first.

He let me turn around then. He was tall and moon-faced. He asked, "What've we got here, Gino?"

Gino grunted. Moon-face ran a hand over my clothes and felt my badge. Then he laughed. It was a full, clear laugh and the little room rang with it. He took a wallet from his pocket and handed it to me.

I read it and laughed, too. I reached down for the .45 and nobody minded.

Lafferty (that's what it said on his identification) said, "Isn't there trouble enough about local and federal government without city police and the FBI playing cops-and-robbers with each other?"

I said, "That's all right. But what'a a G-man doing stooging for a black-market operator?"

He grinned. "Put it the other way round. Gino's our stooge, and a hell of a good one. I thought you were from the gang he's working with. Someday, God help him, they're going to get wise."

Gino showed three and a half teeth. "Your country free mine from Nazis. I help."

Lafferty asked, "And what did you want with him?"

I told him. When I was through I said to Gino, "And what were you doing with Flaxner?"

"One of the black-market boys see him, tell me he use to work with Johnny Angelino, maybe he work with us. I feel him out; he tell me he think about it."

I can't help it; routine's routine. I asked, "And where were you last night at seven-forty?"

Lafferty said, "With me, making out a report."

"That leaves *me* with a ghost."

Lafferty shook his head. "I'm not trying to run your business, Lieutenant; but doesn't it look as if there never was a trick-or-treater? It's a put-up job."

I said, "I've heard terror in a woman's voice before.

Rose Flaxner's mortally afraid of what she saw. And I'm beginning to be myself."

Back at the office I read the report from Richmond. Helen Kirk arrived at work on time last night—eight o'clock. From South Berkeley to there in twenty minutes isn't possible. And the clocks, they swore, can't be faked.

I was left with the ghost, all right.

I hunted out the mask and the sheet. They didn't tell anything. A sheet is shapeless and sizeless. So's a mask. There was no laundry mark on the sheet and no makeup inside the mask. The lab hoped it could do something with identification from sweat-groups; but the courts aren't sold on that one yet, and, anyway, first I'd have to make a pinch.

I tucked the mask under my arm.

I went to every house in a five-block radius of the Flaxners' store. I asked every mother did her kid go trick-or-treating last night. And if the answer was yes, I said what time did he get home and was he all right or did anything funny happen to him.

They mostly got home at nine if they were due at eight, and ten if they were due at nine. And nothing happened.

Until at last on Ellsworth Street a Mrs. Mary Murdock, housewife, said Terry got home before eight. It worried her; he was so early. And he had terrible nightmares last night and was so upset this morning he didn't go to school. It wasn't like Terry; he wasn't one of these sensitive children.

I said, "Lady, it wouldn't take a sensitive kid to have nightmares, if what I think happened. Could I use your phone?"

When I was through phoning I went in to see Terry. I showed him my badge and we talked shop. He was a Junior G-man and he knew some things I didn't. When everything was going smooth, I let him see the mask.

It took me ten minutes to quiet him down, and then I got the story, after I promised he could wear my badge all day, because nothing could get him then.

I had them all there when I walked into the Flaxners' store. Rose was sniffling and nervous. Joe was comforting her like a big brother, only not quite, and Helen

Kirk was watching them. Gino and Lafferty sat apart, saying nothing.

I walked in and said, "Well, I've found him."

Rose sat up and asked, "Who?" as if she was afraid of the answer.

I said, "The trick-or-treat. The one that rang the doorbell last night."

Rose half-screamed. She said, "You can't. He's dead."

I walked back to the door and fetched in the kid. I said, "This is Terry. He—"

I didn't get any further, because just then Lafferty, following my suggestions on the phone, quickly and carefully shot the gun out of Joe Flaxner's hand.

"Gee, it was awful," Terry told us. This was after the squad car took Joe away. "There I was ringing the doorbell, and all of a sudden there was this Thing behind me. It was just like what I was playing at being was all of a sudden real, and it was too big. And the man opened the door and the Thing fired at him and he fell down holding his stomach, and then the Thing grabbed me in its long arms and ran away. And when we were out of sight, it told me not to say a word ever or it'd come and get me the way it got him. I ran all the way home and I felt funny all night."

I said, "Joe was smart. His scheme meant we'd be looking for a little killer, and his height alibied him. But he wasn't smart; he should've picked a better witness than Rose. Only the fact that I believed she was really scared to death kept me from throwing the whole story out. She was a natural for an accessory, and I'm still not too sure—"

"I'll show you," Rose said wildly. "I wouldn't help— a murderer. I'll even tell you where the gun went."

She did, and then I said, "Now I'll tell you. I'll give you five to one it's this rod right here that Joe pulled today. I'm pretty sure that San Francisco train story was a gag to make you think he was the big strong man to rely on in time of murder."

Lafferty said, "Okay. But what put you on the trail of Joe?"

I said, "It wasn't the ghost, I hoped, and it wasn't Helen Kirk and it wasn't Gino. Their alibis stood up. So it wasn't under five feet. So it wasn't the trick-or-treat. So it used a real trick-or-treat for its front. So find the one that got scared last night.

"It had to be Joe. He had a strong motive—it was obvious he wanted Rose—and no alibi. And it *was* Joe. You know, it's the damnedest thing: nine times out of ten, it just naturally is the guy it has to be."

The trail was easy. The gun was almost enough, but Terry's identification of the voice and even the sweat-type testimony helped. And Joe's big, silent, tough-guy act didn't help him, not even with Rose.

I was some worried about Terry. So was his mother, and for a while she didn't like me much. But once he found out it wasn't a Thing, but just a murderer, like any Junior G-man can take in his stride, it was all right. In fact, the last time I saw him he was mad at me. I wouldn't try to get him a ticket to Joe's execution.

THE OCTOBER GAME

by Ray Bradbury

Ray Bradbury (1920–), one of America's most talented and famous writers, has been entertaining millions of readers since the 1940s with his stories. Among his most popular collections are The Illustrated Man *(1951),* The Golden Apples of the Sun *(1953),* A Medicine for Melancholy *(1959), and the definitive* The Stories of Ray Bradbury *(1980). Some of his favorite subjects include youth, the dark, and holidays.*

He put the gun back into the bureau drawer and shut the drawer.

No, not that way. Louise wouldn't suffer that way. She would be dead and it would be over and she wouldn't suffer. It was very important that this thing have, above all, duration. Duration through imagination. How to prolong the suffering? How, first of all, to bring it about? Well.

The man standing before the bedroom mirror carefully fitted his cuff links together. He paused long enough to hear the children run by swiftly on the street below, outside this warm two-story house; like so many gray mice the children, like so many leaves.

By the sound of the children you knew the calendar day. By their screams you knew what evening it was. You knew it was very late in the year. October. The last day of October, with white bone masks and cut pumpkins and the smell of dropped candle fat.

No. Things hadn't been right for some time. October didn't help any. If anything it made things worse. He adjusted his black bow tie. If this were spring, he nodded slowly, quietly, emotionlessly at his image in the mirror, then there might be a chance. But tonight all the world was burning down into ruin. There was no

44

green of spring, none of the freshness, none of the promise.

There was a soft running in the hall. "That's Marion," he told himself. "My little one. All eight quiet years of her. Never a word. Just her luminous gray eyes and her wondering little mouth." His daughter had been in and out all evening, trying on various masks, asking him which was most terrifying, most horrible. They had both finally decided on the skeleton mask. It was "just awful!" It would "scare the beans" from people!

Again he caught the long look of thought and deliberation he gave himself in the mirror. He had never liked October. Ever since he first lay in the autumn leaves before his grandmother's house many years ago and heard the wind and saw the empty trees. It had made him cry, without a reason. And a little of that sadness returned each year to him. It always went away with spring.

But it was different tonight. There was a feeling of autumn coming to last a million years.

There would be no spring.

He had been crying quietly all evening. It did not show, not a vestige of it, on his face. It was all somewhere hidden, but it wouldn't stop.

A rich syrupy smell of candy filled the bustling house. Louise had laid out apples in new skins of caramel, there were vast bowls of punch fresh mixed, stringed apples in each door, scooped, vented pumpkins peering triangularly from each cold window. There was a waiting water tub in the center of the living room, waiting, with a sack of apples nearby, for bobbing to begin. All that was needed was the catalyst, the inpouring of children, to start the apples bobbing, the stringed apples to penduluming in the crowded doors, the candy to vanish, the halls to echo with fright or delight, it was all the same.

Now the house was silent with preparation. And just a little more than that.

Louise had managed to be in every other room save the room he was in today. It was her very fine way of intimating, Oh look, Mich, see how busy I am! So busy that when you walk into a room *I'm* in, there's always something I need to do in *another* room! Just see how I dash about!

For a while he had played a little game with her, a nasty childish game. When she was in the kitchen, then he came to the kitchen, saying, "I need a glass of water." After a moment, he standing, drinking water, she like a crystal witch over the caramel brew bubbling like a prehistoric mudpot on the stove, she said, "Oh, I must light the window pumpkins!" and she rushed to the living room to make the pumpkins smile with light. He came after her, smiling, "I must get my pipe." "Oh, the cider!" she had cried, running to the dining room. "I'll check the cider," he had said. But when he tried following, she ran to the bathroom and locked the door.

He stood outside the bath door, laughing strangely and senselessly, his pipe gone cold in his mouth, and then, tired of the game, but stubborn, he waited another five minutes. There was not a sound from the bath. And lest she enjoy in any way knowing that he waited outside, irritated, he suddenly jerked about and walked upstairs, whistling merrily.

At the top of the stairs he had waited. Finally he had heard the bath door unlatch and she had come out and life belowstairs had resumed, as life in a jungle must resume once a terror had passed on away and the antelope return to their spring.

Now, as he finished his bow tie and put on his dark coat, there was a mouse-rustle in the hall. Marion appeared in the door, all skeletonous in her disguise.

"How do I look, Papa?"

"Fine!"

From under the mask, blond hair showed. From the skull sockets, small blue eyes smiled. He sighed. Marion and Louise, the two silent denouncers of his virility, his dark power. What alchemy had there been in Louise that took the dark of a dark man and bleached and bleached the dark brown eyes and black black hair and washed and bleached the ingrown baby all during the period from birth until the child was born, Marion, blond, blue-eyed, ruddy-cheeked? Sometimes he suspected that Louise had conceived the child as an idea, completely asexual, an immaculate conception of contemptuous mind and cell. As a firm rebuke to him she had produced a child in her *own* image, and, to top it, she had some-how *fixed* the doctor so he shook his head and said, "Sorry, Mr. Wilder, your wife will never have another child. This is the *last* one."

"And I wanted a boy," Mich had said, eight years ago.

He almost bent to take hold of Marion now, in her skull mask. He felt an inexplicable rush of pity for her because she had never had a father's love, only the crushing, holding love of a loveless mother. But most of all he pitied himself, that somehow he had not made the most of a bad birth, enjoyed his daughter for herself, regardless of her not being dark and a son and like himself. Somewhere he had missed out. Other things being equal, he would have loved the child. But Louise hadn't wanted a child, anyway, in the first place. She had been frightened of the idea of birth. He had forced the child on her, and from that night, all through the year until the agony of the birth itself, Louise had lived in another part of the house. She had expected to die with the forced child. It had been very easy for Louise to hate this husband who so wanted a son that he gave his only wife over to the mortuary.

But—Louise had lived. And in triumph! Her eyes the day he came to the hospital were cold. I'm alive, they said. And I have a *blond* daughter! Just look! And when he had put out a hand to touch, the mother had turned away to conspire with her new pink daughter-child—away from the dark forcing murderer. It had all been so beautifully ironic. His selfishness deserved it.

But now it was October again. There had been other Octobers and when he thought of the long winter he had been filled with horror year after year to think of the endless months mortared into the house by an in-sane fall of snow, trapped with a woman and a child, neither of whom loved him, for months on end. During the eight years there had been respites. In spring and summer you got out, walked, picnicked; these were des-perate solutions to the desperate problem of a hated man.

But in winter, the hikes and picnics and escapes fell away with the leaves. Life, like a tree, stood empty, the fruit picked, the sap run to earth. Yes, you invited peo-

ple in, but people were hard to get in winter with bliz-
zards and all. Once he had been clever enough to save
for a Florida trip. They had gone south. He had walked
in the open.

But now, the eighth winter coming; he knew things
were finally at an end. He simply could not wear this
one through. There was an acid walled off in him that
slowly had eaten through tissue and tissue over the
years, and now, tonight, it would reach the wild explo-
sive in him and all would be over!

There was a mad ringing of the bell below. In the
hall, Louise went to see. Marion, without a word, ran
down to greet the first arrivals. There were shouts and
hilarity.

He walked to the top of the stairs.

Louise was below, taking wraps. She was tall and
slender and blond to the point of whiteness, laughing
down upon the new children.

He hesitated. What was all this? The years? The
boredom of living? Where had it gone wrong? Certainly
not with the birth of the child alone. But it had been a
symbol of all their tensions, he imagined. His jealousies
and his business failures and all the rotten rest of it.
Why didn't he just turn, pack a suitcase, and leave?
No. Not without hurting Louise as much as she had
hurt him. It was simple as that. Divorce wouldn't hurt
her at all. It would simply be an end to numb indecision.
If he thought divorce would give her pleasure in any
way he would stay married the rest of his life to her,
for damned spite. No, he must hurt her. Figure some
way, perhaps, to take Marion away from her—legally.
Yes. That was it. That would hurt most of all. To take
Marion away.

"Hello down there!" He descended the stairs, beam-
ing.

Louise didn't look up.

"Hi, Mr. Wilder!"

The children shouted, waved as he came down.

By ten o'clock the doorbell had stopped ringing, the
apples were bitten from stringed doors, the pink child
faces were wiped dry from the apple bobbing, napkins
were smeared with caramel and punch, and he, the
husband, with pleasant efficiency had taken over. He

took the party right out of Louise's hands. He ran about talking to the twenty children and the twelve parents who had come and were happy with the special spiked cider he had fixed them. He supervised "Pin the Tail on the Donkey," "Spin the Bottle," "Musical Chairs," and all the rest, midst fits of shouting laughter. Then, in the triangular-eyed pumpkin shine, all house lights out, he cried, "Hush! Follow me!" tiptoeing toward the cellar.

The parents, on the outer periphery of the costumed riot, commented to each other, nodding at the clever husband, speaking to the lucky wife. How *well* he got on with children, they said.

The children crowded after the husband, squealing.

"The cellar!" he cried. "The tomb of the witch!"

More squealing. He made a mock shiver. "Abandon hope all ye who enter here!"

The parents chuckled.

One by one the children slid down a slide that Mich had fixed up from lengths of table-sections, into the dark cellar. He hissed and shouted ghastly utterances after them. A wonderful wailing filled the dark pumpkin-lighted house. Everybody talked at once. Everybody but Marion. She had gone through all the party with a minimum of sound or talk; it was all inside her, all the excitement and joy. What a little troll, he thought. With a shut mouth and shiny eyes she had watched her own party, like so many serpentines, thrown before her.

Now the parents. With laughing reluctance they slid down the short incline, uproarious, while little Marion stood by, always wanting to see it all, to be last. Louise went down without his help. He moved to aid her, but she was gone even before he bent.

The upper house was empty and silent in the candleshine.

Marion stood by the slide. "Here we go," he said, and picked her up.

They sat in a vast circle in the cellar. Warmth came from the distant bulb of the furnace. The chairs stood on a long line down each wall, twenty squealing children, twelve rustling relatives, alternately spaced, with Louise down at the far end. Mich up at this end, near the stairs. He peered but saw nothing. They had all groped to their chairs, catch-as-you-can in the black-ness. The entire program from here on was to be enacted in the dark, he as Mr. Interlocuter. There was a child scampering, a smell of damp cement, and the sound of the wind out in the October stars.

"Now!" cried the husband in the dark cellar. "Quiet!" Everybody settled.

The room was black black. Not a light, not a shine, not a glint of an eye.

A scraping of crockery, a metal rattle.

"The witch is dead," intoned the husband.

"Eeeeeeeeeeeeee," said the children.

"The witch is dead, she had been killed, and here is the knife she was killed with."

He handed over the knife. It was passed from hand to hand, down and around the circle, with chuckles and little odd cries and comments from the adults.

"The witch is dead, and this is her head," whispered the husband, and handed an item to the nearest person.

"Oh, I know how this game is played," some child cried, happily, in the dark. "He gets some old chicken innards from the icebox and hands them around and says, 'These are her innards!' And he makes a clay head and passes it for her head, and passes a soupbone for her arm. And he takes a marble and says, 'This is her eye!' And he takes some corn and says, 'This is her teeth!' And he takes a sack of plum pudding and gives that and says, 'This is her stomach!' I know how *this* is played!"

"Hush, you'll spoil everything," some girl said.

"The witch came to harm, and this is her arm," said Mich.

"Eeeee!"

The items were passed and passed, like hot potatoes, around the circle. Some children screamed, wouldn't touch them. Some ran from their chairs to stand in the center of the cellar until the grisly items had passed by them and on to the next child.

"Aw, it's only chicken insides," scoffed a boy. "Come back, Helen!"

Shot from hand to hand, with small scream after scream, the items went down the line, down, down, to be followed by another and another.

"The witch cut apart, and this is her heart," said the husband.

Six or seven items moving at once through the laughing, trembling dark.

Louise spoke up: "Marion, don't be afraid; it's only play."

Marion didn't say anything.

"Marion?" asked Louise. "Are you afraid?"

Marion didn't speak.

"She's all right," said the husband. "She's not afraid."

On and on the passing, the screams, the hilarity.

The autumn wind sighed about the house. And he, the husband, stood at the head of the dark cellar, intoning the words, handing out the items.

"Marion?" asked Louise again, from far across the cellar.

Everybody was talking.

"Marion?" called Louise.

Everybody quieted.

"Marion, answer me. Are you afraid?"

Marion didn't answer.

The husband stood there at the bottom of the cellar steps.

Louise called, "Marion, are you there?"

No answer. The room was silent.

"Where's Marion?" called Louise.

"She was here," said a boy.

"Maybe she's upstairs."

"Marion!"

No answer. It was quiet.

Louise cried out, "Marion, Marion!"

"Turn on the lights," said one of the adults.

The items stopped passing. The children and adults sat with the witch's items in their hands.

"No." Louise gasped. There was a scraping of her chair, wildly, in the dark. "No. Don't turn on the lights, don't turn on the lights, oh, God, God, God, don't turn them on, please, please *don't* turn on the lights, *don't!*" Louise was shrieking now. The entire cellar froze with the scream.

Nobody moved.

Everyone sat in the dark cellar, suspended in the suddenly frozen task of this October game; the wind blew outside, banging the house, the smell of pumpkins and apples filled the room with the smell of the objects in their fingers while one boy cried, "I'll go upstairs and look!" and he ran upstairs hopefully and out around the house, four times around the house, calling, "Marion, Marion, Marion!" over and over and at last coming slowly down the stairs into the waiting, breathing cellar and saying to the darkness, "I can't find her."

Then . . . some idiot turned on the lights.

HALLOWEEN GIRL

by Robert Grant

Robert Grant lives in Oklahoma, and is a newspaper correspondent and farmer. "Halloween Girl" is his first published story.

"The Frankenstein monster?"

"Too common."

"Dracula?"

"Doesn't look monsterish enough."

"The Phantom of the Opera?"

"Well..."

"Werewolf?"

"Now you're talking!"

It was decided, then. Tommy would be a werewolf, a furred and fanged slinker in the darkness, claws glistening in the full moon's light. Marcie had already settled on being a mummy.

They were sprawled on the back porch of Marcie's house, their schoolbooks dumped to one side, their eyes riveted to the magazine before them: *Famous Monsters of Filmland.*

"Well, I'm glad that's settled," said Marcie. "About time, too. There's not that much time left, and it's only the most important thing of all."

Tommy waved a lazily buzzing fly away from his blond hair. "Have you finished the skulls yet?"

"Sure. All but the dripping blood. We can paint it on together."

As they talked, as they planned, the great dreadful marvelous day seemed as close as their own breath. So few days, short days getting shorter, racing and rushing by, and the Night loomed close, too close for breathing room. The black and orange celebration, the eve of dancing witches and moaning skulls, of howling things and silently creeping things. The night when darkness took on a shape and walked about, wrapping its melancholy cape about you and bidding you go forth with it for the great party of eternal midnight.

Tommy and Marcie looked forward to it with a fever of longing, more than to Christmas even, because it linked them in a special way. It was the different holiday—not all sparkling lights and radiant smiles, but dark and secretive and strange, gleeful in a grisly way—and they were different, too. Different from all the other kids, not by choice but naturally and irrevocably, in the marrow of their dreams.

The friendship had just happened, as things will when they must. Marcie's family had moved to town a little more than a year ago, and Tommy, who had never thought much about girls one way or another, hadn't paid particular attention to the new auburn-haired pupil with the eyes that wanted to give friendship but always danced away like a deer in a forest.

Then their fourth-grade class had to give oral reports on short stories, and when Tommy's choice was "The Premature Burial" and Marcie's "The Damned Thing," the link was forged. After class he had found himself asking, "You like those kinds of stories?"

And so it had gone. A mutual interest—no, a feeling, a surging need for the fantastic, the ghoulish, the shadows that lurked inside shadows. Heedless of their classmates' teasing ("Look who's in love!"), they seemed always to be together. When a new horror movie came to town, they would be side by side in the candy-scented darkness on Saturday afternoon, and they haunted the fantasy-jammed wonderland of the comic book racks. But their favorite province, their kingdom, was the hushed aisle of the library, where they fearlessly ventured into the dark regions of the grown-up section. For there lurked *Frankenstein, Dracula, Dr. Jekyll and Mr. Hyde,* and their brethren.

When not unearthing what netherworldly treasures their small town had to offer, they would be at their hidden sanctum, behind a ramshackle storage shed in Tommy's backyard. There, in a small shaded spot, invisible to the dull outsiders, they pored over their ghastly booty and poured out their souls, both emptying their own magics, the shared wonderful strangeness that was theirs alone while the rest of the world threw balls, kicked tin cans, and went on its own gray way.

"Boy, they really goofed in that scene where the vampire went out in daylight!"

"No lie!"

And:

"I think 'The Call of Cthulhu' is better because you have to imagine what the monster looks like. It's eerie that way."

"Yeah, but 'The Whisperer in Darkness' has a better ending."

And:

"Boy, we're gonna make a haul this year! Last Halloween my bag was nearly overflowing with candy bars and caramels and bubble gum and licorice and—"

"Licorice, ugh! I always throw mine away."

"Marcie! How could you! Well, this year you can throw it into my sack."

And so it went. Afternoons flew by on batwings, riding a high howling wind of imagination that bore them above the plain white houses and the dismal green classrooms and the endless flat grasslands.

Now the bond had become more intense, more centered as the Night of Nights approached. There were so many things to do, so much making and searching and assembling so that the splendid ceremony of laughing darkness would be right in every detail.

Marcie applied paints and crayons and scissors, conjuring forth superbly horrid creatures that soon glowered at their windows. Tommy gathered wood and cloth and cardboard, which became scarecrow phantoms and witches and demons, unblinking sentries for their front porches.

Together they kept watch on the dime store, where the ritual talismans gradually appeared: masks with malignant leers frozen in plastic; costumes cut from the fabric of night itself; and such atmosphere-completing ornaments as plastic jack-o'-lanterns and witch-shaped candles.

But most of all, they mingled their dreams of the coming night, pooling fantasies, relishing already how it would be: the shadows rushing past as they made their journey, moving in new horrible forms through the dark that bustled with fellow visitors from the elder domains. Up to each house, up to each porch, up to each door they would fly, demanding their booty, the sacrifice, the offering that alone could spare the household from evil.

They would talk here behind the shed until the sun threatened to quench itself in a last cool blaze that played fiery among the crisping leaves. Then Marcie would sigh, rise, and go.

"See you."

"Yeah, okay."

And after his partner in goblins and yearning had gone, Tommy would sit for a while watching the autumn's golden blood grow cooler and dimmer, playing with their dreams a bit more before going into the house.

One morning Marcie didn't meet Tommy in front of school as always. She wasn't in class for roll call. All day Tommy pondered her absence; she had been fine the previous afternoon. They had planned to inspect pumpkins at the grocery store today.

After school Tommy walked straight to Marcie's house. Her mother answered the door and said Marcie had become sick in the night. She was sorry, she said, but he couldn't see her just now. She was sorry, but things were so upset there was no time to say much. She was sorry...

On his way home Tommy noticed vaguely, through his numbness, what a nice day it was. The air was surprisingly warm, a vagrant echo of a summer that had gone away somewhere. Yet there was no question that the weather wasn't young anymore. Beyond the trees, beyond the horizon, something chilly and gray lay waiting.

A week passed with Marcie's desk at school empty. Tommy still could not see her. All he knew, all that he could snatch from the half-overheard conversations of his parents and the maddeningly uninformative soothing was that she was not better.

Tommy floated listlessly through the days, trying not to imagine. He sat stonily in class; he roamed to familiar places out of habit, not thinking much of where he was. Mostly he hid behind the storage shed. He wasn't sure from what he was hiding, but it was something beyond his control, something fearsome but perhaps more sad than mean.

He tried not to imagine.

Nine days after Marcie's first absence Tommy came home from school, and his parents quietly asked him to come into the living room and sit down.

He went in ahead of them, a strange immense emptiness opening in him, an emptiness that had to be there because if you let anything come in, if you thought or felt, it would be dangerous. You'd let in something sharp and terrible and final.

But his parents' words, no matter how cushioned, would be not denied entrance. They came in, telling what his heart knew already, and with them came a cold, rolling, growing blackness that was too big, too filling. Its relentless fullness ached and pressed until it spilled in great knifing sobs through which a thought lanced: I never even got to see her...

After the first spasm of grief, he relieved his parents by his composure, his outward acceptance. In the days that followed, Tommy was unusually quiet, but not grim, not depressed. He went to school, came home, did his homework, loafed about, read, and watched television. When a friend asked him over or when his parents proposed an outing, he seemed uninterested, but it was not a morbid turning away into a private misery. He never had been an outgoing boy.

So by the time Halloween arrived, all who had observed him anxiously for signs of prolonged mourning were satisfied that he had adjusted nicely in a very short time.

Tommy didn't consider for a moment not going out that night. If anything, he was determined to go; there was an aspect of duty to it, of remembrance, even of tribute. He expected no fun. The joy, the spectral exaltation so long promised, would not be there. No use to look for it in the ritual, for it had been broken into pieces and swept away into some dark unreachable place. But he had to go.

Alone. His parents suggested making the rounds with

some others, but Tommy declined softly. It had to be just him, alone riding the night like a gigantic black cat, the night they should have shared. That joy wouldn't happen now, but to be in the midst of outsiders' laughter, pretending to be one of them, would make it worse.

So into the night he went, a plastic-faced werewolf carrying an empty bag.

Through the dark October maze of leaf-strewn lawns and bleak streets, glowing porches looming up where doors would open and someone would make a polite comment on one's costume and then hold forth a hand from which dimly discerned objects would patter into one's bag. House after house, street after ghostly street, the lamps on the corners adding lunar circles in the sky. All about were noises—laughter just ahead, scurrying footsteps across the street, muffled voices coming and going, elusive firefly voices.

It was close under the mask; Tommy's breath came back to him, and his forehead was damp. He made his way steadily, methodically. No running, not catching the night, the whole orange and black event from house to house, a slow solitary figure—he rapped at the doors almost reticently, gently spoke the three-word incantation and just as gently thanked the tall strangers before returning to the blackness with his ever heavier bag.

His path wound from familiar streets that now looked strange into neighborhoods that were new to him. Anonymous houses with nameless people inside, people with the same faces and voices over and over, each adding to his bounty. Was this his town? In the big timeless night he could be anywhere, he could be wandering lost through nightmare streets and alleys that led nowhere. In his warm monster's cocoon he didn't care, he didn't think, he just continued because...because he had to.

At some point Tommy realized that he had stopped walking. That he was no longer in the midst of houses. That he stood before a stone wall that vanished into the night in both directions. The only sound was a hint of breeze-whispered leaves.

A high iron gate was there, and before Tommy knew quite why, he had slipped his grass-blade form through two bars, and now stood alone, awesomely alone, at the edge of a seemingly infinite level expanse of grassy land. There were the occasional shadowy shapes of trees and neatly cut bushes, and there were many stone markers of every size and form.

Knowing where he was, knowing that what had brought him was something deeper and stronger than conscious intent, Tommy walked past the rows of stone objects, his path a web of wan moonlight and tangled shadows.

Suddenly it was there, waiting for him in the muted pearliness, the smaller marker standing forlorn but faithful.

Tommy sat down on the ground, holding the loaded sack in his lap, and removed his mask.

"I went out," he said. "I knew you'd want me to. I'm a werewolf, just like we decided."

He swallowed, fingering the string of the mask. "It was okay, I guess. Lots of kids out. I didn't see anyone we knew. 'Course it's hard to tell when they're all dressed up."

He shifted to a reclining position on his side, laying the bag next to him. Leaves and breezes made dry, distant sounds somewhere.

"I got plenty of stuff. I haven't taken a look at it yet. Mrs. Edwards gave popcorn balls like always."

The surrounding shadows seemed to breathe gently, silently across the void overhead. Tommy grasped for more words, but all that came was an immense yearning. The emptiness, the vast incompleteness that he had held down for so long and so desperately rose up and seized him in its draining downward pull.

"Marcie, it wasn't okay. It was awful. It wasn't fun, it just wasn't anything because you weren't there with me, you were here with the... with the..."

Like a lighted candle in a jack-o'-lantern, something dawned inside him, something that felt like understanding. He thought he'd gone out into the Halloween night for *her*, danced the witches' dance for her, reaped the grisly October harvest because she couldn't.

But now he knew that it was she who had gone into the night for him. She had led the way into the secret heart of midnight. She was a part of it now, she *was*

Halloween in a way he couldn't be with his plastic mask from the dime store.

Finally, now, the tears came. Not mourning tears, but October tears that fell as naturally and with the same necessity as falling leaves. The warm wet drops were lost in a strange wind out of the night as Tommy laid his sack by the small stone marker.

"Thanks, Marcie," he whispered. Then he turned and went back the way he had come, through the gate and toward the town, his home, his bed.

He awoke to the tentative sunlight of an autumn morning and to a strange smell. Actually, it was a combination of two smells—a melancholy one of moist earth, and a happy one of dark, inviting sweetness.

As the sleep left his eyes, he noticed with a dawning smile the three long black objects laid neatly beside his pillow.

"I forgot," he murmured. "I forgot you didn't like licorice."

DAY OF THE VAMPIRE

by Edward D. Hoch

Edward D. Hoch (1930–) has one of the longest bibliographies of any living writer. In the space of less than thirty years, he has written and sold well over six hundred stories, the vast majority to mystery magazines. His gigantic output is of remarkably high quality and is focused around some fifteen separate series, very little of which has been collected. He is a master practitioner of the locked-room impossible-crime story, and delights in the formal detective tale. He served as President of the Mystery Writers of America from 1982 to 1983.

The first thing a visitor saw on the main street of Kreen Falls was the large red, white, and blue banner that stretched from the second floor of Santon's Drugstore to the Odd Fellows' Hall across the way. There were crescent-shaped holes in its fabric to let the wind through, and it was hopefully high enough from the street to avoid the tops of the giant trailer-trucks that rolled through the town too often these days.

Frank Creasley was proud of his banner. It had cost his campaign fund nearly two hundred dollars, but it was the biggest thing they'd ever seen across the main street of Kreen Falls. *Keep Creasley Sheriff*, it read. *Our Lawman Deserves a Fourth Term!* At least once a day during the warm October, he would walk along the street and stop to gaze up at it with a sort of childish awe.

"Checking the sign, Frank?" Tom Santon asked him one morning, standing in the drugstore doorway. Tom was fifty, balding, and practically blind without his thick glasses, but he was the only druggist in Kreen Falls, a position that almost automatically made him one of the town's leading citizens.

"It looks good, Tom," Sheriff Creasley told him. "It's going to get me reelected."

"You'd get reelected without the sign. After all, who else is there?"

It was true, and Creasley knew it. The only opposition was an ex-state trooper named Jack England, a young man whose campaign tactics thus far had centered around cleverly snide remarks about the size of Creasley's stomach. Jack England may have had youth on his side, but he had little else to put up against six years of Sheriff Creasley's daily walks down Main Street.

"Tom, I feel good today. Don't need any of your pills, but I might be back later for some of your coffee." He waved a hand in casual leave-taking and continued his stroll down the street.

Off in the distance, a few blocks down Main Street, he could see the changing color of the leaves. The warmth of October had lingered late, and this year the leaves would barely be on the ground in time for the Halloween bonfires. Kids were a big problem in Kreen Falls—always had been. They read the big city newspapers and got ideas. Bonfires on Halloween were the least of it, and a sheriff with a big stomach couldn't run as fast as he once did.

"Sheriff Creasley!"

He turned and saw the thin, pale-faced figure of Donald Quest bearing down on him. Quest looked like the local undertaker, and he was. "How are you, Don? Beautiful day. Just enough breeze to move my banner a little."

"I've got troubles, sheriff." Don Quest looked both ways, as if fearing he was being followed.

"What kind, Don? Did you lose a body?"

"Remember that bum you found out on Canyon Road last night?"

Creasley remembered. A dead man next to the highway; fairly routine. They hadn't even bothered with an autopsy. After all, why waste the taxpayers' money figuring out how a bum died? "What about him, Don?"

"I was starting to embalm the body, and . . . Sheriff, there's no blood in it."

Creasley blinked. "What are you trying to say, Don?"

"I'm telling you! The blood was drained out of him.

All of it! Just like in those vampire movies on television."

Sheriff Creasley cursed silently and turned his back on the election banner over Main Street to follow Quest.

At the funeral parlor, Quest hovered over the naked corpse on the slotted table with all the flair of a master chef. "See?" he said. "Just like I said."

Creasley took one quick look at the body, then turned away. He'd never gotten used to the messier parts of his job. "Why would anybody take his blood?" he asked distastefully.

"Them vampires do it all the time."

"Sure. Vampires in Kreen Falls. And two weeks before election!" Creasley turned back to the body. "His skin's sure a funny color."

"The lack of blood did that. I should have noticed it sooner."

"What do we do now?" Sheriff Creasley asked, feeling somewhat at a loss.

"I think we should contact the state police. They have a criminal investigation section, don't they?"

Creasley scratched his head. "I can't call them in, Don. You know Jack England's an ex-trooper. How would that look to the voters?"

The pale undertaker shook his head. "I don't know, sheriff."

"Who else did you tell about this?"

"Nobody. I came looking for you first thing, sheriff."

Creasley turned away for a moment, staring at the whitewashed wall of the basement workroom. Finally he said, "Forget about it, Don. Bury him and forget about it."

"Do you think we should?"

"He was only a bum. Whatever happened to him, it doesn't matter now."

Jack England was a handsome man in his early thirties. His tanned face and pale blue eyes somehow gave the impression of steel-hard certainty, and his speeches had just the right quality to build on that image. He'd been a highway patrolman with the state police until he cracked up his car one night chasing a speeder. Left with a slight limp that would have retired him to a desk job, he quit the troopers to try his hand at politics back home. The party figured him a natural candidate to oppose fat and balding Frank Creasley for sheriff, and the campaign was shaping up as one of the roughest in the mild history of Kreen Falls elections.

Sheriff Creasley himself often turned up at Jack England's campaign speeches, standing near the back of the crowd and smiling an oblique approval when the scattered booing of England started. Creasley was still the more popular of the two men, especially among the Main Street merchants who saw him daily.

This night, with a cold chill of autumn beginning to make itself felt, England was speaking from the back of a truck in the parking lot of the town's only shopping center. Creasley remained in his own car, but with the window open so he could hear the vibrant voice of his opponent over the rasping public-address system.

"Do you want," Jack England was asking, "the kind of horse-and-buggy sheriff's department Frank Creasley has given you for six years? Do you want Kreen Falls to remain the laughingstock of the state with its caricature of an overweight sheriff with an underweight brain?" A few boos broke out at these final words, but not as many as Creasley had expected, and he shifted uneasily in his seat. "Don't take a chance with your safety, your children's safety. Vote for modern, progressive law enforcement on election day!" England concluded his speech and acknowledged the tide of applause.

Frank Creasley watched the proceedings for another few minutes and then drove away. He did not drive home but went instead to the little apartment over a Main Street grocery store.

Helen Varro answered his knock and stood aside with a sardonic smile. "I expected you earlier," she told him. "Were you out listening to England's speeches again?"

"He's getting the crowds. And the cheers."

"You're worried." She made the words an accusation.

"Not really." He kissed her lightly on the cheek. Sometimes he wished he'd met Helen Varro twenty years earlier, when he could have legalized their relationship with a wedding ring instead of profaning it with a bottle of Scotch.

"Thanks," she said simply, accepting the bottle and going into the kitchen for some glasses. Helen was a tall, slender girl with dark hair and perfect legs. She worked in one of the county offices during the day, and that was where Frank Creasley had met her. "But you are worried."

"About Jack England? His kind come and go. I've got the people on my side."

Helen came back with glasses generously full of ice cubes and Scotch. "Would they stay on your side if there were a big crime—like a murder or a bank robbery?"

Frank Creasley felt a chill run down his spine. Until that moment he'd forgotten the dead bum by the side of the road. "I suppose," he answered slowly, "a smart guy like England might even try to plant a crime on me."

She handed him a glass and then joined him on the couch. "How could he do that?" she asked.

"There are ways. Let's not worry about it tonight, though. Did you see my banner over Main Street?"

"How could I miss it?"

"It's good for votes. Makes me look like a big man."

"You are a big man, Frank. You could be a bigger one if you really tried."

"What's that supposed to mean?"

"You could start by getting out of Kreen Falls. It's a big state."

Creasley sighed and reached for his glass. "I'm happy here, Helen. You know that. Ten years ago I was a young punk trying to sell real estate. Today I'm the sheriff. Maybe that's as far as I can ever go."

"You're happy because you've got a wife at home and me up here, because there's no crime to speak of in Kreen Falls, and because it's an easy job of chasing kids and running for reelection every two years."

He sighed again. "What do you want me to do?"

"Get out of Kreen Falls, lose some weight, and make a name for yourself!"

"And take you with me," he said, completing her thought.

"Frank—"

"I know, I know." He slipped his arms around her, and for a short time he really believed the things she said about him.

Then, on the way home, he stopped to look at the banner again, softly rippling in the night breeze, and he knew this was as far as he would ever get.

Donald Quest, looking uneasy, sat across the table from Sheriff Creasley. They were in the back of Santon's Drugstore by the soda fountain, with two half-finished cups of coffee on the marble tabletop between them.

"So what's on your mind, Don?" Creasley asked in his early-morning mood.

"It's like this, sheriff." The slim undertaker cleared his throat. "I've been running into lots of heavy expenses lately. New equipment, that new hearse..."

"So?"

"Anyway, I need some money, sheriff. I need to borrow some money."

"Try the bank."

"I thought I'd ask you first, sheriff."

"I can't help you, Don."

"Three hundred dollars would get me out of a bad hole."

"I don't have three hundred, Don. You should know that."

The undertaker shifted his coffee cup restlessly. "I was thinking about that body last week, sheriff. The fellow without any blood."

"What about him?"

"I took an awful chance just burying him like that, without even reporting it."

"You reported it. You reported it to me."

"Yeah, but—"

"Don, if you've got something to say to me, you'd better come out with it. I've got a busy day."

"Don't get touchy, sheriff. It's just that I'm in a hole. I need about three hundred—"

"Or you'll go running to Jack England with your story. Is that what you're trying to say?"

"No! No! I—"

"I thought we were friends, Don."

"We are!"

Creasley stood up and started to leave the table. Then, as an afterthought, he tossed down a couple of dimes for the coffee. The coins clattered and bounced on the marble top, and one of them landed on the floor. He didn't bother to pick it up.

Arnie Banter was the county political leader, a sad-faced man who'd built a chain of gasoline stations into a minor power base of sorts. The upstate politicians might dismiss him with a knowing smirk, but in certain circles of Kreen Falls his words still carried weight. Sitting in his little office on Main Street, Creasley was aware that he was in the presence of the boss.

"I'm getting reports," Arnie said slowly. "Jack England is on to something he's going to spring against you."

Creasley shifted in his chair. "He'd better hurry up. The election's next Tuesday."

Tom Santon, the druggist, and a couple of other local politicians were crowded into the office, too. They were all looking too somber for this late in the campaign.

"This is no fooling, Frank," Santon told him. "I've heard the same thing. He's going to spring something in tonight's speech at the shopping center."

"We'd better pray for rain," Creasley said, taking out a cigar.

Banter's eyes hardened for just an instant. "I don't intend to lose any elections to Jack England's crowd."

"You won't."

"You got any idea what he might have against you?"

Creasley gazed thoughtfully out the window. By stretching a bit in his chair he could just see a corner of the banner, drooping in the unmoving afternoon air. "No idea at all. Probably some phony charge."

"We'll see," Arnie said, still looking unhappy.

Frank Creasley found the undertaker in his basement, scrubbing down the great table with its tubes and attachments. "Hello, sheriff. I didn't hear you come in."

Creasley stepped in very close to the thin man. "Hear this, then, Quest. What in hell have you told Jack England, and how much did he pay you for it?"

"What?"

The sheriff slapped him across the face, not too hard. "You heard me. What did you tell him?"

"I didn't mean any harm. But I *told* you I was short of cash. I came to you first, remember?"

"Yeah." Creasley turned and left the basement room, suddenly unable to stand the smell of it any longer.

He walked down Main Street in a sort of fog, not even bothering to look up at his banner, seeking only the comfort of some dark cave where he might be safe from the hounds that would follow. He found it at Helen Varro's apartment, where he sat looking out the window until she returned from the office.

"What's the matter?" she asked as she entered, catching the anxious lines around his eyes.

"Jack England. He's going to say something in his speech tonight."

"What about?"

"He gave Don Quest, the undertaker, some money to say that I'm covering up a mysterious death. Some bum was found out on the highway a couple of weeks ago, and Quest claims there was no blood in his body."

"Is it true?"

"Is anything ever true during an election campaign? Quest was trying to shake me down. He probably drained the blood out of the body himself. Then he made up a crazy story about vampires!"

"Then it *did* happen, Frank."

"Look," he said with a sigh, "do you think there's a vampire loose in Kreen Falls?"

She smiled at that. "Of course not, but there are forms of insanity. I read about a murderer in England, just a while back, who drank the blood of his victims. You could drive into the city and talk to a psychiatrist about it," Helen suggested.

"Nuts."

"It might be important, Frank. You shouldn't have tried to cover the thing up."

"You're against me, too. You're sounding just like them."

"Are you going to hear England's speech?"

He glanced at the clock on the bare wall. "I suppose so. Come with me, Helen."

"All right."

They took her car and drove out to the shopping center, and it was much like the other nights except that the crowd might have been a bit larger, a little more on edge. The word had gotten around.

Jack England was late, but when he finally put in his appearance, a cheer went up that echoed against the big glass front of the supermarket. Creasley noticed that his hair was rumpled, and his smile seemed a bit tired. "First of all," he began, "I want to thank all you good people for waiting for me like this. It shows you're interested in what I've got to say, and I'm not going to disappoint you!"

Another car pulled up behind Creasely and Helen. He saw Tom Santon at the wheel, and Arnie was with him.

"No," the voice went on, "I'm not going to disappoint you! I have here, in my hand, the sworn affidavit of Donald Quest. You all know our undertaker, one of the leading citizens of Kreen Falls. You know him as a man you can trust to speak the truth. Well, this is Donald Quest's story: A couple of weeks back, the body of a man—since identified as an unemployed migrant worker—was found beside the state highway a few miles out of town. There was only a small wound on the body, and it was assumed that death was caused by a heart attack. The body was turned over to Quest."

Creasely asked Helen for a cigarette and lit it. The guy was good. He was getting the crowd worked up with his drawn-out account of what had happened. "Damn him," Creasley said. "Why didn't he stick to talking about my stomach?"

"He's giving you a battle, Frank. This year it's not going to be enough to walk up Main Street shaking hands."

Creasely grunted and started listening to England again. "...the *sheriff*, the very man who is asking for reelection to his post next Tuesday! Ladies and gentlemen, if there is a madman loose in Kreen Falls, a murderer who drinks human blood, I will not feel safe in my bed until Frank Creasley is replaced as sheriff of Kreen Falls!"

Creasely snorted and ground out the half-smoked

cigarette. "A murderer who drinks human blood! Nuts!" He got out of Helen's car and went over to speak with Santon and Arnie. "All right, there he is! You heard it?"

Arnie was looking unhappy. "Did you tell Quest to bury the body and forget it?"

"Of course not! The whole thing's a damned lie."

"They'll dig up the body and check," Tom Santon warned.

"Let them! His veins are full of embalming fluid now. It won't prove a thing."

Arnie looked up quickly. "It's your word against his, huh?"

"That's correct."

"All right. Just watch your step, Frank. We want a winner next Tuesday."

"You've got one."

He walked back to Helen's car and slid in beside her. "Let's go home," he said quietly.

The psychiatrist was a middle-aged man with an unpronounceable German name and tired eyes that seemed to reflect the daily uncertainties of city life. He stared at Sheriff Creasley, taking in the suit coat that no longer quite buttoned over the stomach, and said, "Vampires? Is that it?"

"Vampires. What can you tell me about them, doctor?"

The psychiatrist turned and walked over to the window, seeming to stare through the grillwork at the farthest wing of the rambling building. "Well, we have never recorded a case of vampirism here at the state hospital, but there are records of such things."

"People turning into bats, stakes through the heart, that sort of thing?"

"Hardly, sheriff." He pulled down a fat volume from the bookshelf and flipped through a few pages. "But vampirism as a special form of insanity—a form of advanced sadism, if you will—is not unheard-of. There was the case of a sailor named James Brown, back in 1867, who killed two shipmates and drank their blood. Later, I believe, he also killed a fellow prisoner at an asylum in the same manner. Some reports credit the

English murderer Christie with having drunk the blood of his victims, and there are similar recorded cases from other countries. It happens, though rarely."

"It doesn't happen in my town."

"There was Peter Kurten, the Dusseldorf murderer," the doctor hurried on. "And a man in Portugal named Salvarrey. That was in 1910. Both confessed to drinking their victims' blood."

"You believe this stuff, doctor?"

"It happened. If you are so doubtful, why did you come to me in the first place?" he asked.

Creasley scratched his head. "A friend wanted me to, but I guess I'm on the wrong track. We've got nobody like that in Kreen Falls."

"Can you be so sure, sheriff?"

"I know my people. I've spent a lifetime knowing them. Maybe they get drunk on a Saturday night, or even steal a car once in a while, but they don't kill people and drink their blood."

The psychiatrist removed his glasses and began to polish them with the corner of his handkerchief. "Very well," he said. "I hope I've been of some assistance."

"Yeah. Thanks anyway."

Frank Creasley was happy to be out of the somber old building and on his way back to Kreen Falls and the people he understood.

"I'll speak tomorrow night," he told Helen later, at her apartment. "I'll answer their charges."

"That'll be a good night for it."

"Why?"

"It's Halloween."

A misty sort of drizzle that had hung over the town in the morning gave way gradually to a warming sunshine in the afternoon, and children already masked and costumed for the night ahead were busy checking the dampness of leaf piles for possible later burning.

Sheriff Creasley saw it all as he strolled down Main Street to Santon's Drugstore. The people he passed were still friendly, but there seemed about them now a note of uncertainty, a vague feeling that all was not quite right. He felt like shaking them, telling them *he* was not this thing they feared, telling them there were no vampires in Kreen Falls.

"Morning, Tom," he greeted the druggist.

Santon finished locking his drug cabinet and came out from the back of the shop. "Arnie says you're speaking tonight."

"Right. I was thinking I could hold the rally right here, in front of your store."

"Here?"

Creasley nodded. "You've got that little balcony upstairs, right where my banner is attached. I was thinking I could speak from there, with the banner for sort of a background. Get everybody to see it."

Santon shrugged. "Everybody's seen it already. Yesterday a truck driver had to go around the block because he couldn't get under it. But you can use the balcony if you want. Only thing is, you'll have to climb out of my storeroom window. There's no door."

"That's all right. We'll make it for about eight-thirty. I'll tell Arnie to start spreading the word."

"Won't it block the traffic?"

Sheriff Creasley chuckled. "That's one way of getting a crowd."

He left the drugstore and walked back down Main Street to Helen Varro's apartment. He knew he should call his wife to tell her about the rally, but somehow he resisted the impulse. She'd never added anything to his political life.

"Will you be there tonight?" he asked Helen.

"You know I will. Tell me what you're going to say."

He went over to her, slipping his arm around her shoulder. "Helen, you're the only one who really cares about me. Sometimes I wonder why you keep it up. I'm fat and dumb, and married besides."

"Maybe I see something in you the others don't, Frank. Maybe I see you leaving this place and making a name for yourself."

He smiled down at her. "That again? Where else would people vote for a fat, dumb guy like me?"

"There are plenty of fat, dumb voters around, Frank. Never forget that."

Her doorbell gave an uncertain tingle, and Creasley turned toward it curiously. "Who can that be?"

"I'll go see."

The man standing in the hallway was tall and hand-some, with pale blue eyes set in a deeply tanned face. They both knew him, too well. It was Jack England. "May I come in?" he asked.

Creasley stepped into view. "Is this another of your cheap campaign tactics, England? Raiding a love nest or something like that?"

The younger man blinked. "I had to speak with you and this seemed a likely place. It needn't be mentioned, by me or anyone else."

Creasley nodded a bit uncertainly. "What do you want?"

Jack England glanced at Helen without speaking, and she took the hint. "Let me get you both a drink," she said.

"Just coffee for me, please," England said. Then, when Helen had disappeared into the kitchen, he began to speak, quietly, intently. "Sheriff, I won't pretend that I admire or even respect you. I'm going to do my damnedest to defeat you next Tuesday. But I find I have to appeal to you on this vampire business."

"Appeal to me?"

"Look, sheriff, you know better than anyone else that Quest's story is true. This thing is more than just pol-itics. There's a madman loose in this town."

"A vampire?" Creasley asked with a thin smile. "I doubt that."

"Then what do you think the explanation is?"

"I could almost think, England, that your people got a dead body from somewhere and faked the whole thing. But I'm more inclined to the belief that Quest did it as part of a shakedown scheme."

"Is that what you're going to tell the people in your talk tonight?"

"Something like that, yes."

Jack England frowned. "Donald Quest is a strange man. Sure, he tried to shake you down, and he did get money from my people, but he deeply resents this talk that he's lying. Right now he's quite bitter against you."

"Let him be."

"You won't work with me to find this madman?"

"There is no madman. One body doesn't make a madman."

Jack England stood up. "Suppose I told you there'd been others."

"Other what?"

"Other mysterious deaths. Not here, but around this part of the state."

"With the blood gone?"

"Not all of it. But there were a couple of bodies— migrant workers again—that seemed to have lost a great deal of blood from wounds. Maybe our man just got greedy with this last one and took it all."

"Nuts."

"That's all you've got to say?"

"You'll hear the rest of it tonight."

Jack England sighed. "Very well."

Helen came back in as the door was closing. "He left without his coffee," she said.

"I guess he wasn't thirsty after all."

The crowd began to gather early, a motley assortment of costumed children and topcoated adults, their breaths visible in the chill evening air. Somewhere far down the street a bonfire was raging, and shop windows along Main Street were already being streaked with irregular trails of soap.

Frank Creasley pushed by a tiny, witch and made his way into Santon's Drugstore at exactly twenty minutes after eight. He said a few words to the druggist and Arnie, accepted a good-luck handshake from the latter, and then climbed the stairs to the second floor. Arnie Banter climbed out the window after him, and they stood together looking down at the crowd on Main Street. Above him, almost touching his shoulder, Creasley's banner flapped gently in the breeze. Arnie had hired a spotlight to shine on it and help attract a crowd.

Below, on the opposite sidewalk, Creasley saw Helen standing in a doorway. He scanned the crowd for Jack England, too, but his rival was nowhere to be seen.

"Ladies and gentlemen of our fine community!" He paused after that opening line, waiting for the noise to die down. A distant siren sounded as the volunteers went after another bonfire. "Ladies and gentlemen! I come before you tonight, almost on the eve of the election, to set the record straight! I have been accused by my opponent of a terrible thing—of trying to cover up a murder. Most of you have known me all your lives, and I hope you recognized that charge for the dirty lie it is!" He leaned against the flimsy balcony railing, staring down hard at them. Yes, there was England. He'd come after all.

"Donald Quest, the undertaker of Kreen Falls, has attempted a truly foul crime. More than a week ago he sat downstairs in this very drugstore and demanded money from me. When I refused him, he sold his pack of lies to the opposition."

Behind him, Arnie gasped something. Creasley turned and saw the little undertaker climbing out the window, a look of something like madness in his eyes. "And here he is! Here he is, folks! Do you believe in vampires, or do you believe in foul-mouthed scum like Don Quest?"

"Stop it!" Quest shouted above the crowd's roar. "Stop it! Tell them the truth, sheriff. Tell them the truth!" He seemed close to tears as he screamed the words.

Creasley held his ground, while Arnie tried to get a grip on the undertaker. "I have told them the truth, Quest."

The little man broke free from Arnie and hurled himself forward. "Damn you!"

What happened next was so sudden that Creasley moved only by reflex. He stepped aside, reaching out to Arnie for support, as Donald Quest stumbled past him and hit the flimsy railing. The wood crunched and gave way, and in a final desperate lunge the undertaker managed to grip the very edge of the great cloth banner. It started ripping slowly, and then all at once collapsed under his weight.

That should have been enough to break his fall and save his life, but it wasn't. The crowd scattered as he hung dangling above them, and when he landed he hit the old stone curbing headfirst.

On Wednesday morning Frank Creasley strolled along Main Street, feeling good. He went into Santon's Drugstore and called out a cheerful good morning.

"You did it," Santon said, coming out to shake his hand. "Almost two thousand votes!"

Creasley smiled. "Only sixteen hundred, really. I think the final tally was 5,237 to 3,601. But it was enough. It was enough, Tom."

The druggist polished away a speck on the counter. "You know what I think, Frank? I think when Quest died like that, they thought it was sort of an act of God."

"Maybe. Life is funny sometimes. Seen England around?"

Santon shook his head. "Probably sleeping it off somewhere."

Creasley nodded and went back outside. He stood for a moment breathing in the brisk November air, then turned in the direction of Helen's apartment.

After the sheriff had gone, Tom Santon unlocked his drug cabinet and carefully removed a large bottle of reddish liquid from the cooling compartment. He stood gazing at it for some time before he finally, reluctantly, replaced it.

Creasley was still the sheriff of Kreen Falls, and he, Santon, would be safe here a little longer.

NIGHT OF THE GOBLIN

by Talmage Powell

*Talmage Powell (1920–) lives in North Carolina and
is the author of ten novels and over five hundred short
stories and screenplays. Among his works are* Corpus
Delectable *(1964),* The Girl Who Killed Things *(1960),*
The Killer is Mine *(1959), and* Start Screaming Murder
(1962).

Bobby palmed the packet of razor blades and dropped
his hand in his pocket as he sidled on toward the candy
racks. It was the first time in his eight years he'd stolen
anything, and he had the sudden sickening expectancy
of sirens and flashing lights.

He dawdled at the tier of small bins holding candy
bars while the feverish upsurge of guilty sweat cooled
on his forehead. Two other people were in the neighborhood convenience store, a woman paying for a bottle
of milk and loaf of bread, and Mr. Pepper, the pleasant
old man who clerked in the store.

As the woman went out, Bobby chose a Karmel King,
crossed to the counter, and dropped a coin from his
damp palm.

"Hi, young fella!" Mr. Pepper, as always, had a
warm smile for Bobby. Sometimes, when traffic was
slow, they would chat while Bobby sipped a soda pop.
The old man seemed forever fascinated, delighted, be-
mused by Bobby's wit, intelligence, and scope of knowl-
edge. Kids nowadays...smarter than scientists used
to be...weaned on moon walks, fourth dimensions,
space warps, atomic fission, computers, TV classrooms,
nuclear bombs...Saganian witchcraft...

Bobby supposed that Mr. Pepper had to work because
his social security wouldn't keep up with inflation. He
wondered what it was like to be old.

"Guess you'll go trick-or-treat tonight, Bobby."

Bobby nodded, his throat a bit dry. With the razor blades in his pocket, he didn't want to linger in the tall gray presence.

"Halloween ain't what it used to be." Mr. Pepper held Bobby's Karmel King in one hand, Bobby's coin in the other. "When I was a boy Halloween was a kind of street carnival, folks dressing up like spooks and pirates and swarming through the streets of old downtown. You might get your face throwed full of flour, or have somebody drop a paper sack full of water on your head from an upstairs window. Merchants got their store windows all soaped over, and if you didn't take the swing off the front porch you might find it atop a lamppost next morning. It was a night for turning over outhouses and letting the air out of tin lizzie tires—but there weren't the creeps around to drug or poison the stuff dropped in a little child's trick-or-treat sack."

"Please, sir ... You don't have to bother putting my Karmel King in a bag." Bobby took the candy bar, and fled.

Jethro "Jet" Simmons, lead guitar with the rock group Iceberg, lately employed six nights at the Asphalt Cowboy Disco, slouched in the recliner and watched the quarterback keep the ball on an option play. The TV commentator explained that it was an option play with the quarterback keeping the ball, which brought a sneer to Jet's thin lips. Bunch of dumb creeps, those sports announcers.

"Hey, Judy," he yelled, dropping the empty beer can on the chairside table, "make with a brew."

"I just brought you the last one from the fridge," Judy Clark called from a bedroom.

"Be a kitten," Jet called back, "and get us a six-pack. The goons are right in the middle of the second quarter."

Judy appeared in the inner doorway of the small living–dining room. "And I'm up to my elbows in black crepe paper, trying to fashion some sort of little-old-man suit, pants and jacket yet, to hang together for one evening."

In their deep sockets, Jet's moody eyes frosted. "Why the hell can't the kid put on a bedsheet and be a ghost, like any normal kid? All this crap about turning into a gnome, a goblin for Halloween..."

"His heart's set on it, Jet. You know kids at Bobby's age. Things that don't matter to grown-ups can be terribly important to them. He's a good boy, and Halloween is only one night out of the year. Is it asking so much?"

Who wants to know kids, Jet asked himself tightly, especially the brat by her ex-husband that Judy should have aborted the day after she missed her period. Little fink. No tantrums. No open challenges. Just that glint of wisdom and hatred Jet sometimes caught in the bright brown eyes.

But two can play that game, brat. Pretense and smiles.

While the quarterback threw an incomplete forward pass, Jet stretched, yawned, stood up. He was tall, lean, pantherishly muscled, with a rawboned face framed in shoulder-length waves of glossy brown. He washed his hair at least once a day and enjoyed drying and brushing it out. He was equally vain of the flatness of his belly, the leanness of hips in his brushed denims, the biceps that bulged the short sleeves of his black knitted shirt.

"Grab a six-pack at the convenience store during the halftime break," Judy suggested. Trim, attractive, the emerald softness of her eyes highlighted by the deep auburn of her hair, she worked five days a week as a respiratory therapist in the huge hospital nearby. Robert, her husband, had walked out three years ago. ("Sorry, nothing personal, Judy; just up to here with the marriage bit. You can tell Bobby I went off to the wars, or something.") Great for the ego. She hadn't heard from Robert since.

"And while you're buying the beer," Judy added, "pick up a Karmel King candy bar. It's Bobby's favorite, and it would be nice if you dropped it into his trick-or-treat bag yourself, Jet."

Her gaze lingered on the closed door after Jet went out. He had moved into the apartment across the hall two months ago. They'd met a week later, coming into the building, and a thing had quickly developed. Last week Jet had carried his personal belongings, guitar and amplifier, clothing, stereo, tennis racket, barbells across the corridor into her apartment.

Even though the arrangement was acceptable nowadays, Judy had suffered a twinge of conscience, due to a somewhat old-fashioned upbringing and her deep love for Bobby.

A block away, Ed Travis walked into his kitchen. In paint-splotched work pants and T-shirt, he had worked up a steamy sweat even though October was closing on a crisp autumn note. He yanked a paper towel from the holder beside the sink and mopped his craggy face. He was a big, powerful man, feline in his movements in the way of a leopard. A plainclothes detective, he was devoting several off-duty hours to wedge and sledge, bursting down to wood-stove size the sawn circular sections of oak tree trunk piled in his backyard. Wheelbarrow load at a time, he was stacking the firewood neatly alongside the garage. Piecemealing the job over the next few weeks he'd have plenty for the winter, and the fuel oil dealer could spit in the tank.

Blond and slender, so very perfect for his dark heft, Marian was at the kitchen table arranging the punchbowl set as a centerpiece for the trays of Halloween cookies. She glanced over her shoulder, smiling. "I'll bet I know someone who could use something tall and cool and wet."

Marian turned toward the refrigerator, poured an iced-tea glass almost full of orange juice, leaving room for a couple of ice cubes and a half-inch of sour mash whiskey.

She handed Ed the finished drink, and he sank onto a kitchen chair with a pleasantly tired grunt. He took a long pull and exhaled gustily. "Now, that's a drink for the old woodsman!"

"How's it going?"

"Fine. About another half-cord cut and stacked today. Guess I'll knock off. Have a good, hot bathtub and get ready for dinner. Potluck?"

"You know it."

Ed looked at the homemade cookies iced in greens, oranges, blacks. He wondered if he could get away with eating a couple of the little chocolate jack-o'-lanterns?

Probably. But Marian had the trays so beautifully arranged. He let his stomach rumble, unrequited.

"How many kids you taking trick-or-treat?"

Marian shrugged. "All that show up by seven-thirty. Esther and I invited the eight close by."

"Probably have a dozen," Travis said. "More the merrier. I got some extra-nice red delicious for the apple dunking when you bring them back here for the party."

"Ed," Marian said, turning to fill the coffee maker, "why the hell don't you give in and eat some jack-o'-lanterns? Plenty more over there on the sideboard."

"You ought to be a parole officer," he said, reaching. "Head off a lot of trouble, way you read impulses in the criminal mind."

"One for me, too," Esther squealed from the doorway. She flashed across the room, climbed up on him, plopped against him. Five years old, her daddy's dark coloration was in her large, happy eyes and hair that lay in soft ringlets. The rest of her, the grace of limb and lovely piquancy of face, was sheer Marian. Ed's heart jumped pleasurably every time he looked at her. If the depth of feeling was a little unmanly, the hell with manliness.

"Cookie yourself," Ed said. "Take a bite out of you!"

He growled ferociously, and Esther wriggled, giggling in delight. They tussled and brawled, Ed tickling her ribs and nibbling the back of her tiny neck while she writhed and filled the kitchen with her laughter, and Marian tossed a fond smile their way.

Finally, Esther fell back against his massive arm, looking up at him, gasping through parted lips. "Daddy, I laughed so hard I almost went t-t in my pants!"

"Well, I'm glad you didn't. Very unladylike. You know, Mama's been so busy doing for this party, why don't we do something for her?"

Esther half raised. "What, Daddy?"

"Go to the fried chicken place and bring back a barrel for dinner. Like a party of our own."

Bobby cleared a spot on the small table in his room by setting his microscope and a box of parts for a half-finished model car temporarily on the floor. He turned on a gooseneck lamp and laid the Karmel King, purchased, and the razor blades, stolen, in the glare.

He tried not to think of the way he'd gotten the blades, while he sat in a straight wooden chair and pulled himself hard against the edge of the table. He picked up the dime store magnifying glass normally used to examine used postage stamps purchased, when affordable, from a dealer's penny–nickle–dime barrel. He laid the Karmel King with the lettered topside of the wrapper against the table, and studied for a moment the way the gold and tan wrapper was folded and sealed.

One of Mommy's old tweezers, stamp tongs, lay beside a perf gauge, amid a clutter, orderly to its owner, of stamp sheets, science fiction comic books, and experiments with a little rubber-type printing machine.

Carefully he inserted a tweezer tine under the imperfectly joined folds in the candy bar wrapper. Lower lip pressed between his teeth, he applied gentle pressure. The fold popped loose. Bobby drew a long breath before attacking the wrapper further.

In a few moments, he had opened the wrapper without marring it with a single tear. The Karmel King lay exposed, dark and naked in its skin of chocolate.

He rested briefly; then he picked up the candy with one hand, a razor blade in the other. Face set in intense concentration, he started at a corner and made a thin cut around the thinner perimeter of the candy bar, along the sides and across the ends. Gently. The chocolate must not chip. The cut must be even and straight.

He repeated the cut, deepening the surgery. The Karmel King came apart in two perfect layers. He eased them onto the table, top and bottom, insides facing the ceiling.

Breathing through his mouth, he cuffed sweat from his forehead with the back of his hand. So far, perfect. Once the halves were rejoined into a whole candy bar, the perimeter cut could easily be wiped away with a careful stroking of a warm thumb along the chocolate surface. Then back into the undamaged wrapper... cautiously preserving the original folds...a touch of model airplane glue to reseal...And no one could tell by looking at the candy bar that it hadn't just come from the factory.

But before that, prior to the restoration, came the part that Bobby dreaded most.

He set his teeth, snapped his head in a shake, and rummaged his needle-nosed pliers from among the tools in the table drawer—wood carving set, small ball peen hammer, screwdriver, jackknife.

He slipped the remaining razor blades from their plastic casing one by one onto the tabletop. With the pliers he broke a blade in half, lengthwise, then into shorter pieces. He embedded a piece vertically into the bottom half of the Karmel King...then another... another...another...working tirelessly while the supply of blades dwindled.

"Bubble, bubble, toil, and trouble," Ed Travis boomed, flinging open the front door, peering through the eyeholes of a Frankenstein monster mask. "What have we here? A witch with an expired broomstick license and her scary helpers with loaded trick-or-treat sacks."

Eight assorted miniature beings from Star Wars, Brothers Grimm, and other folklore trooped into the Travis living room, where a paper donkey was hung for the tail-pinning, an armada of apples floated in an old-time washtub, a white crepe-paper ghost danced in mid-air, a candle inside a jack-o'-lantern cut from a real pumpkin shed unreal light and shadows.

There was Timmy Brock as R2D2, little Cara Norman beneath a skeleton costume, Bucky Steadman an obvious Rip Van Winkle, Laurie Jameson as a witch, Junior Roberts a cowboy without his hi-yo Silver. Ed's own Esther was a black kitty cat, and Bobby Clark had to be, Ed supposed, a gnome in the little-old-man black outfit, wrinkles eyebrow-penciled on his face, a knotted top from a nylon stocking tightly capped on his head to give him the bald look. Chaperoning the group on the trick-or-treat trek, Marian had ventured forth in a commonplace pants suit.

She closed the door as the final child scurried in, looked at Ed's mask and nodded approval. "Quite an improvement."

"Thought you'd like it," Ed said. He slipped the mask off, turned toward the room. "Okay, kids..."

Ed looked at Marian and grinned. The witching hour creatures scattered about the Travis living room, more interested in treasure troves right now than in anything Esther's papa had to say. They peered into trick-or-treat sacks, plunged in their hands, rummaged, popped candies and gum in their mouths.

"Mr. Travis?" said the goblin.

"Yes, Bobby?"

"I've a Karmel King!"

"Great!" Ed smiled at the expression on the gnome face.

Bobby reached up, holding the candy bar. "I would like to share it with Esther."

"Bobby, I'm sure she has more than..."

"Please, sir. My treat. You and Mrs. Travis and Esther are so nice...this party and all..."

The small, extended hand was insistent. Ed laughed. "Sure, Mr. Goblin, I know what you mean."

Ed took the Karmel King and peeled off the wrapper.

"If you break it a little lopsided," the goblin said, "you may give Esther the big half."

Holding the Karmel King between thumbs and fingers, Ed applied mild pressure to pull the semisoft bar apart. Suddenly he yelped, jerking his finger hand free. He stared at the bright, seeping redness on his left thumb, a glowing ruby of blood. The thought seemed foolish, unreal: the candy bar had cut him.

He whirled toward an occasional table and turned on a lamp. In the spill of light, he stretched, pulled, separating the Karmel King carefully. Frowning, Marian stepped to his side. "What is it, Ed?"

He looked up, his face itself a white, vicious Halloween mask. "Razor blades...the damned candy...Marian, somewhere along the trick-or-treat route we've got an absolute sonofabitch! Bobby!"

"Yes, sir?" said the gnome, suddenly bewildered, frightened.

Ed bent his knees to put himself on eye-level. "Have you any idea where you got the Karmel King? Which house, apartment? Who?"

"Yes, sir," Bobby said. "Jet gave it to me."

"Jet?"

"Jethro Simmons, Mr. Travis. He's Mommy's boy-friend."

"I see...Bobby, this is very important. You mustn't

make a mistake. Are you absolutely sure he gave you the Karmel King?"

"You can ask Mrs. Travis," Bobby said. "Jet said, 'Here is your favorite,' and handed me the Karmel King." It was the moment of crisis, showdown, and Bobby was sweating lightly. His mind sparked with the memory of covertly dropping Jet's Karmel King in a street gutter and slipping the candy he'd prepared into his trick-or-treat bag.

"That's right, Ed," Marian said tightly. "Bobby is telling the truth."

"Is that the only Karmel King in your bag?" Ed asked, his detective's mind covering all details.

"Yes, sir, I'm sure it is. But you can look."

Ed spilled the contents of the bag on the table; candy kisses, bubble gums, an apple, cookies, and lollipops.

Ed lifted his stony eyes. "Marian, get me a piece of aluminum foil to wrap this candy in." He glanced about the room. "Sorry . . . it was to be such a fine party . . . Well, they can still have the games and refreshments. Gather up every bit of this trick-or-treat stuff . . . I'm going back on duty as of now . . ."

Bobby lay in the silence of his room looking at the softness of moonlight framed in his window. He shifted on his mattress, thinking of the way Mr. Travis had looked as he'd phoned police headquarters and left the house. Wow! Bobby sure wouldn't want Mr. Travis coming after *him* with that kind of look on his face!

But it was all right. Everything had worked out okay. Aside from the little cut on Mr. Travis's thumb, nobody had got hurt, and it was okay. A goblin's goal is to protect his treasure, and the treasure was safe. Mama was upset, of course, but she would shape up. Grown-ups got over things almost as well as kids.

It was real nice to have Mama alone in the very next room once more.

A splintery, thudding sound from outside caused Bobby to rear upright. He swung his bare feet from the bed and padded to the window.

In the driveway just below lay the ruins of Jet's stereo. A dark, lumpish shadow swooped out and down, falling beside the stereo. Jet's clothing. Mama had opened the window and was throwing all of Jet's things out.

When the guitar hit the driveway cement, it emitted a skirling discord, a ghostly note exactly right for a Halloween midnight.

THE ADVENTURE
OF THE DEAD CAT

by Ellery Queen

*Ellery Queen (Frederic Dannay: 1905–1982, and
Manfred B. Lee: 1905–1971) was one of the most important figures in the mystery field in the twentieth cen-
tury. These two cousins from Brooklyn, who gave their
pen name to their series detective, were an outstanding
novelist team whose dozens of books were almost im-
mediate successes. They also excelled in shorter fiction,
and virtually kept the mystery short story alive in America after the death of the pulps by founding* Ellery Queen's
Mystery Magazine. *Every writer and lover of the field
is deeply in their debt.*

The square-cut envelope was a creation of orange ink
on black notepaper; by which Ellery instantly divined
its horrid authorship. Behind it leered a bouncy hostess,
all teeth and enthusiastic ideas, who spent large sums
of some embarrassed man's money to build a better
mousetrap.

Having too often been one of the mice, he was grate-
ful that the envelope was addressed to "Miss Nikki
Porter."

"But why to me at your apartment?" wondered Nikki,
turning the black envelope over and finding nothing.

"Studied insult," Ellery assured her. "One of those
acid-sweet women who destroy an honest girl's repu-
tation at a stroke. Don't even open it. Hurl it into the
fire, and let's get on with the work."

So Nikki opened it and drew out an enclosure cut in
the shape of a cat.

"I am a master of metaphor," muttered Ellery.

"What?" said Nikki, unfolding the feline.

"It doesn't matter. But if you insist on playing the

mouse, go ahead and read it." The truth was, he was a little curious himself.

"Fellow Spook," began Nikki, frowning.

"Read no more. The hideous details are already clear—"

"Oh, shut up," said Nikki. *"There is a secret meeting of The Inner Circle of Black Cats in Suite 1313, Hotel Chancellor, City, Oct. 31."*

"Of course," said Ellery glumly. "That follows logically."

"You must come in full costume as a Black Cat, including domino mask. Time your arrival for 9:05 P.M. promptly. Till the Witching Hour. Signed—*G. Host.* How darling!"

"No clue to the criminal?"

"No. I don't recognize the handwriting...."

"Of course you're not going."

"Of course I *am*!"

"Having performed my moral duty as friend, protector, and employer, I now suggest you put the foul thing away and get back to our typewriter."

"What's more," said Nikki, "you're going, too."

Ellery smiled his number-three smile—the toothy one. "Am I?"

"There's a postscript on the cat's—on the reverse side. *Be sure to drag your boss-cat along, also costumed.*"

Ellery could see himself as a sort of overgrown Puss-in-Boots plying the sjambok over a houseful of bounding tabbies all swilling Scotch. The vision was tiring.

"I decline with the usual thanks."

"You're a stuffed shirt."

"I'm an intelligent man."

"You don't know how to have fun."

"These brawls inevitably wind up with someone's husband taking a poke at a tall, dark, handsome stranger."

"Coward."

"Heavens, I wasn't referring to myself—!"

Whence it is obvious he had already lost the engagement.

Ellery stood before a door on the thirteenth floor of the Hotel Chancellor, cursing the Druids.

For it was Samain at whose mossy feet must be laid the origins of our recurrent October silliness. True, the lighting of ceremonial bonfires in a Gaelic glade must have seemed natural and proper at the time, and a Gallic grove fitting rendezvous for an annual convention of ghosts and witches; but the responsibility of even pagan deities must surely be held to extend beyond temporal bounds, and the Druid lord of death should have foreseen that a bonfire would be out of place in a Manhattan hotel suite, not to mention disembodied souls, however wicked.

Then Ellery recalled that Pomona, goddess of fruits, had contributed nuts and apples to the burgeoning Halloween legend, and he cursed the Romans, too.

There had been Inspector Queen at home, who had intolerably chosen to ignore the whole thing; the taxi driver, who had asked amiably, "Fraternity initiation?"; the dread chorus of meows during the long, long trek across the Chancellor lobby; and, finally, the reeking wag in the elevator who had tried to swing Ellery around by his tail, puss-pussying obscenely as he did so.

Cried Ellery out of the agony of his mortification: "Never, never, *never* again will I—"

"Stop grousing and look at this," said Nikki, peering through her domino mask.

"What is it? I can't see through this damned thing."

"A sign on the door. IF YOU ARE A BLACK CAT, WALK IN!!!! With five exclamation points."

"All right, all right. Let's go in and get it over with."

And, of course, when they opened the unlocked door of 1313, darkness.

And silence.

"Now what do we do?" giggled Nikki, and jumped at the snick of the door behind them.

"I'll tell you what," said Ellery enthusiastically. "Let's get the hell out of here."

But Nikki was already a yard away, black in blackness.

"Wait! Give me your hand, Nikki."

"*Mister* Queen. That's not my hand."

"Beg your pardon," muttered Ellery. "We seem to be trapped in a hallway...."

"There's a red light down there! Must be at the end of the hall—*eee!*"

"Think of the soup this would make for the starving." Ellery disentangled her from the embrace of some articulated bones.

"Ellery! I don't think that's funny at all."

"I don't think *any* of this is funny."

They groped toward the red light. It was not so much a light as a rosy shade of darkness, which faintly blushed above a small plinth of the raven variety. The woman's cornered the black-paper market, Ellery thought disagreeably as he read the runes of yellow fire on the plinth:

TURN LEFT!!!!!!!!!

"And into, I take it," he growled, "the great unknown." And, indeed, having explored to the left, his hand encountered outer space; whereupon, intrepidly, and with a large yearning to master the mystery and come to grips with its diabolical authoress, Ellery plunged through the invisible archway, Nikki bravely clinging to his tail.

"Ouch!"

"What's the matter?" gasped Nikki.

"Bumped into a chair. Skinned my shin. What would a chair be doing—?"

"Pooooor Ellery," said Nikki, laughing. "Did the dreat bid mad hurt his— *Ow!*"

"Blast this— Ooo!"

"Ellery, where are you? Ooch!"

"Ow, my foot," bellowed Ellery from somewhere. "What is this—a tank-trap? Floor cluttered with pillows, hassocks—"

"Something cold and wet over here. Feels like an ice bucket...Owwwww!" There was a wild clatter of metal, a soggy crash, and silence again.

"Nikki! What happened?"

"I fell over a rack of fire tongs, I think," Nikki's voice came clearly from floor level. "Yes. Fire tongs."

"Of all the stupid, childish, unfunny—"

"Oop."

"Lost in a madhouse. Why is the furniture scattered every which way?"

"How should I know? Ellery, where *are* you?"

"In Bedlam. Keep your head now, Nikki, and stay where you are. Sooner or later a St. Bernard will find you and bring—"

Nikki screamed.

"Thank God," said Ellery, shutting his eyes.

The room was full of blessed Consolidated Edison light, and various adult figures in black-cat costumes and masks were leaping and laughing and shouting, "Surpriiiiiise!" like idiot phantoms at the crisis of a delirium.

O Halloween.

"Ann! Ann Trent!" Nikki was squealing. "Oh, Ann, you fool, how ever did you find me?"

"Nikki, you're looking *wonderful*. Oh, but you're famous, darling. The great E. Q.'s secretary..."

Nuts to you, sister. Even bouncier than predicted. With that lazy, hippy strut. And chic, glossy chic. Lugs her sex around like a sample case. Kind of female who would be baffled by an egg. Looks five years older than she is, Antoine notwithstanding.

"But it's not Trent anymore, Nikki—Mrs. John Crombie. Johnnnny!"

"Ann, you're *married*? And didn't invite me to the wedding!"

"Spliced in dear old Lunnon. John's British—or was. Johnny, stop flirting with Edith Baxter and come here!"

"Ann darlin'—this exquisite girl! Scotch or bourbon, Nikki? Scotch, if you're the careful type—but bourbon works faster."

John Crombie, Gent. Eyes of artificial blue, slimy smile, sunlamp complexion, Olivier chin. British Club and Fox and Hounds—he posts even in a living room. He will say in a moment that he loathes Americah. Exactly. Ann Trent Crombie must have large amounts of the filthy. He despises her and patronizes her friends. He will fix me with the superior British smile and flap a limp brown hand...*Quod erat demonstrandum.*

"I warn you, Nikki," Ann Crombie was saying, "I'm hitched to a man who tries to jockey every new female he meets." Blush hard, prim Nikki. Friends grow in unforeseen directions. "Oh, Lucy! Nikki, do you remember my kid sister Lu—?"

Squeal, squeal. "Lucy Trent! This isn't *you?*"

"Am I grown up, Nikki?"

"Heavens!"

"Lucy's done *all* the party decorating, darling—spent the whole sordid day up here alone fixing things up. Hasn't she done an *inspired* job? But then, I'm so useless."

"Ann means she wouldn't help, Nikki. Just a lout."

Uncertain laugh. Poor Lucy. Embarrassed by her flowering youth, trying hard to be New York...There she goes refilling a glass—emptying an ashtray—running out to the kitchen—for a tray of fresh hot pigs-in-blankets?—*bong!*...the unwanted and gauche hiding confusion by making herself useful. Keep away from your brother-in-law, dear; that's an upstanding little bosom under the Black Cat's hide.

"Oh, Ellery, do come here and meet the Baxters. Mrs. Baxter—Edith—Ellery Queen..."

What's this? A worm who's turned, surely! The faded-fair type, hard used by wedlock. Very small, a bit on the spready side—she let herself go—but now she's back in harness again, all curried and combed, with a triumphant lift to her pale head, like an old thoroughbred proudly prancing in a paddock she had never hoped to enter again. And that glitter of secret pleasure in her blinky brown eyes, almost malice, whenever she looked at Ann Crombie....

"Jerry Baxter, Edith's husband. Ellery Queen."

"Hiya, son!"

"Hi yourself, Jerry."

Salesman, or advertising-agency man, or Broadway agent. The life of the party. Three drinks and he's off to the races. He will be the first to fall in the apple tub, the first to pin the tail on Lucy or Nikki instead of on the donkey, the first to be sick, and the first to pass out. Skitter, stagger, sweat, and whoop. Why do you whoop, Jerry Baxter?

Ellery shook hot palms, smiled with what he hoped was charm, said affably: "Yes, isn't it?" "Haven't we met somewhere?" "Here, here, that's fine for now," and

things like that, wondering what he was doing in a
hotel living room festooned with apples, marshmallows,
nuts, and crisscrossing crepe-paper twists, hung with
grinning pumpkins and fancy black-and-orange cardboard cats, skeletons, and witches, and choked with
bourbon fumes, tobacco smoke, and Chanel No. 5. Some
Chinese lanterns were reeking, the noise was maddening, and merely to cross the room required the prepa-
rations of an expedition, for the overturned furniture
and other impedimenta on the floor—cunningly plotted
to trap groping Black Cats on their arrival—had been
left where they were.

So Ellery, highball in hand, wedged himself in a safe
corner and mentally added Nikki to the Druids and the
Romans.

Ellery accepted the murder game without a murmur.
He knew the futility of protest. Wherever he went, people at once suggested a murder game, apparently on
the theory that a busman enjoys nothing so much as a
bus. And, of course, he was to be the detective.

"Well, well, let's get started," he said gaily, for all
the traditional Halloween games had been played: Nikki
had slapped Jerry Baxter laughingly once and British
Johnny—not laughingly—twice, the house detective
had made a courtesy call, and it was obvious the de-
lightful evening had all but run its course. He hoped
Nikki would have sense enough to cut the *pièce de ré-
sistance* short, so that a man might go home and give
his thanks to God; but no, there she was in a whispery,
giggly huddle with Ann Crombie and Lucy Trent, while
John Crombie rested his limp hand on her shoulder and
Edith Baxter splashed some angry bourbon into her
glass.

Jerry was on all fours, being a cat.

"In just a minute," called Nikki, and she tripped
through the archway—kitchen-bound, to judge from
certain subsequent cutlery sounds—leaving Crombie's
hand momentarily suspended.

Edith Baxter said, "Jerry, get up off that floor and
stop making a darned fool of yourself!" furiously.

"Now we're all set," announced Nikki, reappearing.
"Everybody around in a circle. First I'll deal out these

cards, and whoever gets the ace of spades, *don't let on!*—
because you're the Murderer."

"Ooh!"

"Ann, you stop peeking."

"Who's peeking?"

"A tenner says I draw the fatal pasteboard," laughed
Crombie. "I'm the killer type."

"I'm the killer type!" shouted Jerry Baxter. "Gack-
gack-gack-gack!"

Ellery closed his eyes.

"Ellery! Wake up."

"Huh?"

Nikki was shaking him. The rest of the company
were lined up on the far side of the room from the
archway, facing the wall. For a panicky moment he
thought of the St. Valentine's Day Massacre.

"You go on over there with the others, smarty-pants.
You mustn't see who the murderer is, either, so you
close your eyes, too."

"Fits in perfectly with my plans," said Ellery, and
he dutifully joined the five people at the wall.

"Spread out a little there—I don't want anyone
touching anyone else. That's it. Eyes all shut? Good.
Now I want the person who drew the ace of spades—
Murderer—to step quietly away from the wall—"

"Not cricket," came John Crombie's annoying alto.
"You'll see who it is, dear heart."

"Yes," said Edith Baxter nastily. "The light's on."

"But I'm running this assassination! Now, stop talking, eyes closed. Step out, Murderer—that's it...quietly!
No talking there at the wall! Mr. Queen is *very* bright
and he'd get the answer in a shot just by eliminating
voices—"

"Oh, come, Nikki," said Mr. Queen modestly.

"Now, Murderer, here's what you do. On the kitchen
table you'll find a full-face mask, a flashlight, and a
bread knife. Wait! Don't start for the kitchen yet—go
when I switch off the light in here; that will be your
signal to start. When you get to the kitchen, put on the
mask, take the flashlight and knife, steal back into this
room, and—pick a victim!"

"Oooh."

"Ahhhh!"

"Ee!"

Mr. Queen banged his forehead lightly against the wall. How long, O Lord?

"Now remember, Murderer," cried Nikki, "you pick anyone you want—except, of course, Ellery. He has to live long enough to solve the crime...."

If you don't hurry, my love, I'll be dead of natural causes.

"It'll be dark, Murderer, except for your flash, so even I won't know what victim you pick—"

"May the detective inquire the exact purpose of the knife?" asked the detective wearily of the wall. "Its utility in this amusement escapes me."

"Oh, the knife's just a prop, goopy—atmosphere. Murderer, you just tap your victim on the shoulder. Victim—whoever feels the tap—turn around and let Murderer lead you out of the living room to the kitchen."

"The kitchen, I take it, is the scene of the crime," said Mr. Queen gloomily.

"Uh-huh. And, Victim, as soon as Murderer gets you into the kitchen, scream like all fury as if you're being stabbed. Make it realistic! Everybody set? Ready?... All right, Murderer, soon's I turn this light off, go to the kitchen, get the mask and stuff, come back, and pick your victim. Here goes!"

Click went the light switch. Being a man who checked his facts, Ellery automatically cheated and opened one eye. Dark, as advertised. He shut the eye, and then jumped.

"Stop!" Nikki had shrieked.

"What, what?" asked Ellery excitedly.

"Oh, I'm not talking to you, Ellery. Murderer, I forgot something! Where are you? Oh, never mind. Remember, after you've supposedly stabbed your victim in the kitchen, come back to this room and quickly take your former place against the wall. Don't make a sound; don't touch anyone. I want the room to be as quiet as it is this minute. Use the flash to help you see your way back, but as soon as you reach the wall, turn the flash off and throw flash and mask into the middle of the living room—thus, darling, getting rid of the evidence. Do you see? But, of course, you *can't*." You're in rare form, old girl." "Now, even though it's dark, people, *keep your eyes shut.* All right, Murderer—get set—*go!*"

Ellery dozed....

It seemed a mere instant later that he heard Nikki's voice saying with incredible energy: "Murderer's tapping a victim—careful with that flashlight, Murderer!—we mustn't tempt our Detective *too* much. All right, Victim? Now let Murderer lead you to your doom...the rest of you keep your eyes closed...don't turn ar-...."

Ellery dozed again.

He awoke with a start at a man's scream.

"Here! What—"

"Ellery Queen, you asleep again? That was Victim being carved up in the kitchen. Now...yes!...here's Murderer's flash back...that's it, to the wall quietly...now flash *off!*—fine!—toss it and your mask away...Boom. Tossed. Are you turned around, face to the wall, Murderer, like everybody else? Everybody ready? Llllllights!"

"Now—" began Ellery briskly.

"Why, it's John who's missing," laughed Lucy.

"Pooooor John is daid," sang Jerry.

"My poor husband," wailed Ann. "Jo-hon, come back to me!"

"Ho, John!" shouted Nikki.

"Just a moment," said Ellery. "Isn't Edith Baxter missing, too?"

"My wiff?" shouted Jerry. "Hey, wiff! Come outa the woodwork!"

"Oh, darn," said Lucy. "There mustn't be two victims, Nikki. That spoils the game."

"Let us repair to the scene of the crime," proclaimed Miss Porter, "and see what gives."

So, laughing and chattering and having a hell of a time, they all trooped through the archway, turned left, crossed the foyer, and went into the Crombie kitchen and found John Crombie on the floor with his throat cut.

When Ellery returned to the kitchen from his very interesting telephone chat with Inspector Queen, he found Ann Crombie being sick over the kitchen sink, her forehead supported by the greenish hand of a greenish Lucy Trent, and Nikki crouched quietly in a corner, as far away from the covered thing on the floor as the architect's plans allowed, while Jerry Baxter raced up and down weeping: "Where's my wife? Where's Edith? We've got to get out of here."

Ellery grabbed Baxter's collar and said, "It's going to be a long night, Jerry—relax. Nikki—"

"Yes, Ellery." She was trembling and trying to stop it and not succeeding.

"You know who was supposed to be the murderer in that foul game—the one who drew the ace of spades— you saw him or her step away from the living room wall while the lights were still on in there. Who was it?"

"Edith Baxter. Edith got the ace. Edith was supposed to be the murderer."

Jerry Baxter jerked out of Ellery's grasp. "You're lying!" he yelled. "You're not mixing my wife up in this stink! You're a lying—"

Ann crept away from the sink, avoiding the mound. She crept past them and went into the foyer and collapsed against the door of a closet just outside the kitchen. Lucy crept after Ann and cuddled against her, whimpering. Ann began to whimper, too.

"Edith Baxter was Murderer," said Nikki drearily. "In the game, anyway."

"You lie! You lying—"

Ellery slapped his mouth without rancor and Baxter started to cry again. "Don't let me come back and find any other throats cut," said Ellery, and he went out of the kitchen.

It was tempting to assume the obvious, which was that Edith Baxter, having drawn the ace of spades, decided to play the role of murderer in earnest, and did so, and fled. Her malice-dipped triumph as she looked at John Crombie's wife, her anger as she watched Crombie pursue Nikki through the evening, told a simple story; and it was really unkind of fate—if fate was the culprit—to place Edith Baxter's hand on John Crombie's shoulder in the victim-choosing phase of the game. In the kitchen, with a bread knife at hand, who could blame a well-bourboned woman if she obeyed that impulse and separated Mr. Crombie's neck from his British collar?

But investigation muddled the obvious. The front door of the suite was locked—nay, even bolted—on the inside. Nikki proclaimed herself the authoress thereof, having performed the sealed-apartment act before the game began (she said) in a moment of "inspiration."

Secondly, escape by one of the windows was out of the question, unless, like Pegasus, Edith Baxter possessed wings.

Thirdly, Edith Baxter had not attempted to escape at all: Ellery found her in the foyer closet against which the widow and her sister whimpered. Mrs. Baxter had been jammed into the closet by a nasty hand, and she was unconscious.

Inspector Queen, Sergeant Velie, & Co. arrived just as Edith Baxter, with the aid of ammonium carbonate, was shuddering back to life.

"Guy named Crombie's throat slit?" bellowed Sergeant Velie without guile.

Edith Baxter's eyes rolled over and Nikki wielded the smelling salts once more, wearily.

"Murder games," said Inspector Queen gently. "Halloween," said Inspector Queen. Ellery blushed. "Well, son?"

Ellery told his story humbly, in penitential detail.

"Well, we'll soon find out," grumbled his father, and he shook Mrs. Baxter until her chin waggled and her eyes flew open. "Come, come, madam, we can't afford these luxuries. What the hell were you doing in that closet?"

Edith screamed, "How should I know, you old man?" and had a convulsion of tears. "Jerry Baxter, how can you sit there and—?"

But her husband was doubled over, holding his head.

"You received Nikki's instructions, Edith," said Ellery, "and when she turned off the light you left the living room and went to the kitchen. Or started for it. What did happen?"

"Don't third-degree me, you detective!" screeched Mrs. Baxter. "I'd just passed under the archway, feeling my way, when somebody grabbed my nose and mouth from

behind and I must have fainted because that's all I
knew till just now and Jerry Baxter, if you don't get
up on your two feet like a man and defend your own
wife, I'll—I'll—"

"Slit his throat?" asked Sergeant Velie crossly, for
the sergeant had been attending his own Halloween
party with the boys of his old precinct and was holding
three queens full when the call to duty came.

"The murderer," said Ellery glumly. "The real murderer, dad. At the time Nikki first put out the lights,
while Edith Baxter was still in the room getting Nikki's
final instructions, one of us lined up at that wall stole
across the room, passed Nikki, passed Edith Baxter in
the dark, and ambushed her—"

"Probably intended to slug her," nodded the inspector, "but Mrs. Baxter obliged by fainting first."

"Then into the closet and away to do the foul deed?"
asked the sergeant poetically. He shook his head.

"It would mean," mused Inspector Queen, "that after
stowing Mrs. Baxter in the foyer closet, the real killer
went into the kitchen, got the mask, flash, and knife,
came back to the living room, tapped John Crombie,
led him out to the kitchen, and carved him up. That
part of it's okay—Crombie must have thought he was
playing the game—but how about the assault on Mrs.
Baxter beforehand? Having to drag her unconscious
body to the closet? Wasn't there any noise, any sound?"

Ellery said apologetically, "I kept dozing off."

But Nikki said, "There was no sound, Inspector. Then
or at any other time. The first *sound* after I turned the
light off was John screaming in the kitchen. The only
other *sound* was the murderer throwing the flash into
the middle of the room after he...she...whoever it
was...got back to the wall."

Jerry Baxter raised his sweating face and looked at
his wife.

"Could be," said the inspector.

"Oh my," said Sergeant Velie. He was studying the
old gentleman as if he couldn't believe his eyes—or
ears.

"It could be," remarked Ellery, "or it couldn't. Edith's
a very small woman. Unconscious, she *could* be carried

noiselessly the few feet in the foyer to the closet...by a reasonably strong person."

Immediately Ann Crombie and Lucy Trent and Jerry Baxter tried to look tiny and helpless, while Edith Baxter tried to look huge and heavy. But the sisters could not look less tall or soundly made than nature had fashioned them, and Jerry's proportions, even allowing for reflexive shrinkage, were elephantine.

"Nikki," said Ellery in a very thoughtful way, "you're sure Edith was the only one to step away from the wall while the light was still on?"

"Dead sure, Ellery."

"And when the one you thought was Edith came back from the kitchen to pick a victim, that person had a full mask on?"

"You mean after I put the light out? Yes. I could see the mask in the glow the flash made."

"Man or woman, Miss P?" interjected the sergeant eagerly. "This could be a pipe. If it was a man—"

But Nikki shook her head. "The flash was pretty weak, Sergeant. And we were all in those Black Cat outfits."

"Me, I'm no Fancy Dan," murmured Inspector Queen unexpectedly. "A man's been knocked off. What I want to know is not who was where when, but—who had it in for this character?"

It was a different sort of shrinkage this time, a shrinkage of four throats. Ellery thought, They *all* know.

"Whoever," he began casually, "whoever knew that John Crombie and Edith Baxter were—"

"It's a lie!" Edith was on her feet, swaying, clawing the air. "There was nothing between John and me. Nothing. Nothing! Jerry, don't believe them!"

Jerry Baxter looked down at the floor again. "Between?" he mumbled. "I guess I got a head. I guess this has got me." And, strangely, he looked not at his wife but at Ann Crombie. "Ann...?"

But Ann was jelly-lipped with fear.

"Nothing!" screamed Jerry's wife.

"That's not true." And now it was Lucy's turn, and they saw she had been shocked into a sort of suicidal courage. "John was a...a...John made love to every woman he met. John made love to *me*—"

"To you." Ann blinked and blinked at her sister.

"Yes. He was...disgusting. I..." Lucy's eyes flamed at Edith Baxter with scorn, with loathing, with contempt. "But *you* didn't find him disgusting, Edith."

Edith glared back, giving hate for hate.

"You spent four weekends with him. And the other night, at that dinner party, when you two stole off—you thought I didn't hear—but you were both tight...you begged him to marry you."

"You nasty little blabbermouth," said Edith in a low voice.

"I heard you. You said you'd divorce Jerry if he'd divorce Ann. And John kind of laughed at you, didn't he?—as if you were dirt. And I saw your eyes, Edith, I saw your eyes...."

And now they, too, saw Edith Baxter's eyes—as they really were.

"I never told you, Ann. I couldn't. I couldn't...." Lucy began to sob into her hands.

Jerry Baxter got up.

"Here, where d'ye think you're going?" asked the sergeant not unkindly.

Jerry Baxter sat down again.

"Mrs. Crombie, did you know what was going on?" asked Inspector Queen sympathetically.

It was queer how she would not look at Edith Baxter, who was sitting lumpily now, no threat to anyone—a soggy old woman.

And Ann said, stiff and tight, "Yes, I knew." Then her mouth loosened again and she said wildly, "I knew, but I'm a coward. I couldn't face him with it. I thought if I shut my eyes—"

"So do I," said Ellery tiredly.

"What?" asked Inspector Queen, turning around. "You what, son? I didn't get you."

"I know who cut Crombie's throat."

They were lined up facing the far wall of the living room—Ann Crombie, Lucy Trent, Edith Baxter, and Jerry Baxter—with a space the breadth of a man, and a little more, between the Baxters. Nikki stood at the light switch, the inspector and Sergeant Velie blocked the archway, and Ellery sat on a hassock in the center of the room, his hands dangling listlessly between his knees.

"This is how we were arranged a couple of hours ago, Dad, except that I was at the wall, too, and so was John Crombie...in that vacant space."

Inspector Queen said nothing.

"The light was still on, as it is now. Nikki had just asked Murderer to step away from the wall and cross the room—that is, toward where you are now. Do it, Edith."

"You mean—"

"Please."

Edith Baxter backed from the wall and turned and slowly picked her way around the overturned furniture. Near the archway, she paused, an arm's length from the inspector and the sergeant.

"With Edith about where she is now, Nikki, in the full light, instructed her about going to the kitchen, getting the mask, flash, and knife there, coming back in the dark with the flash, selecting a victim, and so on. Isn't that right?"

"Yes."

"Then you turned off the light, Nikki—didn't you?"

"Yes..."

"Do it."

"D-do it, Ellery?"

"Do it, Nikki."

When the darkness closed down, someone at the wall gasped. And then the silence closed down, too.

And after a moment Ellery's voice came tiredly: "It was at this point, Nikki, that you said "Stop!" to Edith Baxter and gave her a few additional instructions. About what to do after the 'crime.' As I pointed out a few minutes ago, Dad—it's during this interval, with Edith standing in the archway getting Nikki's afterthoughts, and the room in darkness, that the real murderer must have stolen across the living room from the wall, got past Nikki and Edith and into the foyer, and waited there to ambush Edith."

"Sure, son," said the inspector. "So what?"

"How did the murderer manage to cross this room in pitch darkness without making any noise?"

At the wall, Jerry Baxter said hoarsely, "Y'know, I don't have to stand here. I don't have to!"

"Because, you know," said Ellery reflectively, "there wasn't any noise. None at all. In fact, Nikki, you actually remarked in that interval: 'I want the room to be as quiet as it is this minute.' And only a few moments ago you corroborated yourself when you told Dad that the first sound after you turned off the light was John screaming in the kitchen. You said the only other sound was the sound of the flashlight landing in the middle of the room after the murderer got back to the wall. So I repeat: How did the murderer cross this room in darkness without making a sound?"

Sergeant Velie's disembodied bass complained from the archway that he didn't get it at all, at all.

"Well, Sergeant, you've seen this room—it's cluttered crazily with overturned furniture, pillows, hassocks, miscellaneous objects. Do you think *you* could cross it in darkness without sounding like the bull in the china shop? Nikki, when you and I first got here and blundered into the living room—"

"In the dark," cried Nikki. "We bumped. We scraped. I actually fell—"

"Why didn't the murderer?"

"I'll tell you why," said Inspector Queen suddenly. *"Because no one did cross this room in the dark.* It can't be done without making a racket, or without a light—and there was no light at that time or Nikki'd have seen it."

"Then how's it add up, Inspector?" asked the sergeant pathetically.

"There's only one person we know crossed this room—the one Nikki saw cross while the light was on, the one they found in the closet in a 'faint,' Velie. *Edith Baxter!*"

She sounded nauseated. "Oh no," she said. "No."

"Oh yes, Mrs. Baxter. It's been you all the time. You did get to the kitchen. You got the mask, the flash, the knife. You came back and tapped John Crombie. You led him out to the kitchen and there you sliced him up—"

"No!"

"Then you quietly got into that closet and pulled a phony faint, and waited for them to find you so you could tell that cock-and-bull story of being ambushed in the foyer, and—"

"Dad," sighed Ellery.

"Huh?" And because the old gentleman's memory of similar moments—many similar moments—was very green, his tone became truculent. "Now tell me I'm wrong, Ellery!"

"Edith Baxter is the one person present tonight who couldn't have killed John Crombie."

"You see?" moaned Edith. They could hear her panting.

"Nikki actually saw somebody with a flash *return* to the living room after Crombie's death-scream, go to the wall, turn off the flash, and she heard that person hurl it into the middle of the room. Who was it Nikki saw and heard? We've deduced that already—the actual murderer. Immediately after that, Nikki turned up the lights.

"If Edith Baxter were the murderer, wouldn't we have found her *at the wall with the rest of us* when the lights went on? But she wasn't. She wasn't in the living room at all. We found her in the foyer closet. So she *had* been attacked. She *did* faint. She *didn't* kill Crombie."

They could hear her sobbing in a great release.

"Then who did?" barked the inspector. His tone said he was tired of this fancy stuff and give him a killer so he could book the rat and go home and get to sleep.

"The one," replied Ellery in those weary tones, "who was able to cross the room in the dark without making any noise. For if Edith is innocent, only one of those at the wall could have been guilty. And that one had to cross the room."

There is a maddening unarguability about Ellery's sermons.

"But how, son, how?" bellowed his father. "It couldn't be done without knocking *something* over—making *some* noise!"

"Only one possible explanation," said Ellery tiredly; and then he said, not tiredly at all, but swiftly and with the slashing finality of a knife, "I thought you'd try that. That's why I sat on the hassock, so very tired. That's why I staged this whole...silly...scene...."

Velie was roaring: "Where the hell are the lights? Miss Porter, turn that switch on, will you?"

"I can't find the—the damned thing!" wept Nikki.

"The rest of you stay where you are!" shouted the inspector.

"Now drop the knife," said Ellery, in the slightly gritty tones of one who is exerting pressure. "Drop it...." There was a little clatter, and then a whimper. "The only one who could have passed through this jumbled maze in the dark without stumbling over anything," Ellery went on, breathing a bit harder than usual, "would be someone who'd *plotted a route through this maze in advance of the party*...someone, in fact, who'd plotted the maze. In other words, the clutter in this room is not chance confusion, but deliberate plant. It would require photographing the details of the obstacle course on the memory, and practice, plenty of practice—but we were told you spent the entire day in this suite *alone*, my dear, fixing it up for the party."

"Here!" sobbed Nikki, and she jabbed the light switch.

"I imagine," said Ellery gently to the girl in his grip, "you felt *someone* had to avenge the honor of the Trents, Lucy."

PUMPKIN HEAD

by Al Sarrantonio

Al Sarrantonio is a Bronx, New York-based writer whose stories have graced the pages of most of the science fiction and horror magazines. A former assistant editor at a major New York publishing house, he is now a full-time writer.

An orange and black afternoon.

Outside, under baring but still-robust trees, leaves tapped across sidewalks, a thousand fingernails drawn down a thousand dry blackboards.

Inside, a party beginning.

Ghouls loped up and down aisles between desks, shouting "Boo!" at one another. Crepe paper, crinkly and the colors of Halloween, crisscrossed over blackboards covered with mad and frightful doodlings in red and green chalk: snakes, rats, witches on broomsticks. Windowpanes were filled with cutout black cats and ghosts with no eyes and giant *O's* for mouths.

A fat jack-o'-lantern, flickering orange behind its mouth and eyes and giving off spicy fumes, glared down from Ms. Grinby's desk.

Ms. Grinby, young, bright, and filled with enthusiasm, left the room to chase an errant goblin-child, and one blackboard witch was hastily labeled "Teacher." Ms. Grinby, bearing her captive, returned, saw her caricature, and smiled. "All right, who did this?" she asked, not expecting an answer and not getting one. She tried to look rueful. "Never mind, but I think you know I don't *really* look like that. Except maybe today." She produced a witch's peaked hat from her drawer and put it on with a flourish.

Laughter.

"Ah!" said Ms. Grinby, happy.

106

The party began.

Little bags were handed out, orange and white with freshly twisted tops and filled with orange and white candy corn.

Candy corn disappeared into pink little mouths.

There was much yelling, and the singing of Halloween songs with Ms. Grinby at the piano, and a game of "Pin the Tail on the Black Cat." And then a ghost story, passed from child to child, one sentence each:

"It was a dark and rainy night—"

"—and . . . Peter had to come out of the storm—"

"—and he stopped at the only house on the road—"

"—and no one seemed to be home—"

"—because the house was empty and haunted—"

The story stopped dead at the last seat of the first row.

All eyes focused back on that corner.

The new child.

"Raylee," asked Ms. Grinby gently, "aren't you going to continue the story with us?"

Raylee, new in class that day—the quiet one, the shy one with black bangs and big eyes always looking down—sat with her small, grayish hands folded, her dark brown eyes straight ahead like a rabbit caught in a headlight beam.

"Raylee?"

Raylee's thin pale hands shook.

Ms. Grinby got up quickly and went down the aisle, setting her hand lightly on the girl's shoulder.

"Raylee is just shy," she said, smiling down at the unmoving top of the girl's head. She knelt down to face-level, noticing two round fat beads of water at the corners of the girl's eyes. Her hands were clenched hard.

"Don't you want to join in with the rest of us?" Ms. Grinby whispered, a kindly look washing over her face. Empathy welled up in her. "Wouldn't you like to make friends with everyone here?"

Nothing. She stared straight ahead, the bag of candy, still neatly wrapped and twisted, resting on the varnished and dented desk top before her.

"She's a faggot!"

This from Judy Linthrop, one of the four Linthrop girls, aged six through eleven, and sometimes trouble.

"Now, Judy—" began Ms. Grinby.

"Faggot!" from Roger Mapleton.

"A *faggot!*"

Peter Pakinski, Randy Feffer, Jane Campbell.

All eyes on Raylee for reaction.

"A pale little faggot!"

"That's enough!" said Ms. Grinby, angry, and there was instant silence; the game had gone too far.

"Raylee," she said softly. Her young heart went out to this girl; she longed to scream at her, "Don't be shy! There's no reason, the hurt isn't real, I know, I know!" Images of Ms. Grinby's own childhood, her awful loneliness, came back to her, and with them a lump to her throat.

I know, I know!

"Raylee," she said, her voice a whisper in the party room, "don't you want to join in?"

Silence.

"Raylee—"

"I know a story of my own."

Ms. Grinby nearly gasped with the sound of the girl's voice, it came so suddenly. Her upturned, sad little face abruptly came to life, took on color, became real. There was an earnestness in those eyes, which looked out from the girl's haunted, shy darkness to her and carried her voice with them.

"I'll tell a story of my own if you'll let me."

Ms. Grinby almost clapped her hands. "Of course!" she said. "Class"—looking about her at the other child-faces: some interested, some smirking, some holding back with comments and jeers, seeking an opening, a place to be heard—"Raylee is going to tell us a story. A Halloween story?" she asked, bending back down toward the girl, and when Raylee nodded yes she straightened and smiled and preceded her to the front of the room.

Ms. Grinby sat down on her stool behind her desk.

Raylee stood silent for a moment, before all the eyes and the almost jeers and the smirks, under the crepe paper and cardboard monsters and goblins.

Her eyes were on the floor, and then she suddenly realized that she had taken her bag of candy with her, and stood alone clutching it before them all. Ms. Grinby saw it too, and before Raylee began to shuffle her feet and stand with embarrassment or run from the room, the teacher stood and said, "Here, why don't you let me hold that for you until you're finished?"

She took it from the girl's sweaty hand and sat down again.

Raylee stood silent, eyes downcast.

Ms. Grinby prepared to get up, to save her again.

"This story," Raylee began suddenly, startling the teacher into settling back into her chair, "is a scary one. It's about a little boy named Pumpkin Head."

Ms. Grinby sucked in her breath; there were some whisperings from the class, which she quieted with a stare.

"Pumpkin Head," Raylee went on, her voice small and low but clear and steady, "was very lonely. He had no friends. He was not a bad boy, and he liked to play, but no one would play with him because of the way he looked.

"He was called Pumpkin Head because his head was too big for his body. It had grown too fast for the rest of him, and was soft and large. He only had a little patch of hair, on the top of his head, and the skin on all of his head was soft and fat. You could almost pull it out into folds. His eyes, nose, and mouth were practically lost in all the fat on his face.

"Someone said Pumpkin Head looked that way because his father had worked at an atomic plant and had been in an accident before Pumpkin Head was born. But this wasn't his fault, and even his parents, though they loved him, were afraid of him because of the way he looked. When he stared into a mirror he was almost afraid of himself. At times he wanted to rip at his face with his fingers, or cut it with a knife, or hide it by wearing a bag over it with writing on it that said, 'I am me, I am normal just like you under here.' At times he felt so bad he wanted to bash his head against a wall, or go to the train tracks and let a train run over it."

Raylee paused, and Ms. Grinby almost stopped her, but noting the utter silence of the class, and Raylee's absorption with her story, she held her tongue.

"Finally, Pumpkin Head became so lonely that he

decided to do anything he could to get a friend. He talked to everyone in his class, one by one, as nicely as he could, but no one would go near him. He tried again, but still no one would go near him. Then he finally stopped trying.

"One day he began to cry in class, right in the middle of a history lesson. No one, not even the teacher, could make him stop. The tears ran down Pumpkin Head's face, in furrows like on the hard furrows of a pumpkin. The teacher had to call his mother and father to come and get him, and even they had trouble taking him away because he sat in his chair with his hands tight around his seat and cried and cried. There didn't seem to be enough tears in Pumpkin Head's head for all his crying, and some of his classmates wondered if his pumpkin head was filled with water. But finally his parents brought him home and put him in his room, and there he stayed for three days, crying.

"After those three days passed, Pumpkin Head came out of his room. His tears had dried. He smiled through the ugly folds of skin on his face, and said that he wouldn't cry anymore and that he would like to go back to school. His mother and father wondered if he was really all right, but secretly, Pumpkin Head knew, they sighed with relief because having him around all the time made them nervous. Some of their friends would not come to see them when Pumpkin Head was in the house.

"Pumpkin Head went back to school that morning, smiling. He swung his lunch pail in his hand, his head held high. His teacher and his classmates were very surprised to see him back, and everyone left him alone for a while.

"But then, in the middle of the second period, one of the boys in the class threw a piece of paper at Pumpkin Head, and then another. Someone hissed that his head was like a pumpkin, and that he had better plant it before Halloween. 'And on Halloween we'll break open his pumpkin head!' someone else yelled out.

"Pumpkin Head sat in his seat and carefully brought his lunch box up to his desk. He opened it quietly. Inside was his sandwich, made in a hurry by his mother, and an apple and a bag of cookies. He took these out, and also the thermos filled with milk, and set them on the desk. He closed the lunch pail and snapped shut the lid.

"Pumpkin Head stood and walked to the front of the room, carrying his lunch pail in his hand. He walked to the door and closed it, and then walked calmly to the teacher's desk, turning toward the class. He opened his lunch box.

"'My lunch and dinner,' he said, 'my dinner and breakfast.'

"He took out a sharp kitchen knife from his lunch pail.

"Everyone in the classroom began to scream.

"They took Pumpkin Head away after that, and they put him in a place—"

Ms. Grinby abruptly stepped from behind her desk.

"That's all we have time for, Raylee," she interrupted gently, trying to smile. Inside she wanted to scream over the loneliness of this child. "That was a *very* scary story. Where did you get it from?"

There was silence in the classroom.

Raylee's eyes were back on the floor. "I made it up," she said in a whisper.

To make up something like that, Ms. Grinby thought. *I know, I know!*

She patted the little girl on her back. "Here's your candy; you can sit down now." The girl returned to her seat quickly, eyes averted.

All eyes were on her.

And then something that made Ms. Grinby's heart leap:

"Neat story!" said Randy Feffer.

"Neat!"

"Wow!"

Roger Mapleton, Jane Campbell.

As she sat down, Raylee was trembling but smiling shyly.

"Neat story!"

A bell rang somewhere.

"Can it be that time already?" Ms. Grinby looked at the full-moon–faced wall clock. "Why, it is! Time to go home. I hope everyone had a nice party—and remember! Don't eat too much candy!"

A small hand waved anxiously at her from the center of the room.

"Yes, Cleo?"

Cleo, red-freckled face and blue eyes, stood up. "Can I please tell the class, Ms. Grinby, that I'm having a party tonight, and that I can invite everyone in the class?"

Ms. Grinby smiled. "You may, Cleo, but there doesn't seem to be much left to tell, does there?"

"Well," said Cleo, smiling at Raylee, "only that everyone's invited."

Raylee smiled back and looked quickly away.

Books and candy bags were crumpled together, and all ran out under crepe paper, cats, and ghouls, under the watchful eyes of the jack-o'-lantern, into darkening afternoon.

A black and orange night.

Here came a black cat walking on two legs; there two percale sheet ghosts trailing paper bags with handles; here again a miniature man from outer space. The wind was up: leaves whipped along the serpentine sidewalk like racing cars. There was an apple-crisp smell in the air, an icicle-down-your-spine, here-comes-winter chill. Pumpkins everywhere, and a half harvest moon playing coyly with wisps of high shadowy clouds. A thousand dull yellow night-lights winked through breezy trees on a thousand festooned porches. A constant ringing of doorbells, the wash of goblin traffic: they traveled in twos, threes, or fours, these monsters, held together by Halloween gravity. Groups passed other groups, just coming up, or coming down, stairs, made faces, and said "Boo!" There were a million "Boo!" greetings this night.

On one particular porch in all that thousand, goblins went up the steps but did not come down again. The door opened a crack, then wider, and groups of ghosts, wizards, and spooks, instead of waiting patiently for a toss in a bag and then turning away, slipped through into the house and disappeared from the night. Disappeared into another night.

Through the hallway and kitchen and down another set of stairs to the cellar. A cellar transformed. A cellar of hell, this cellar—charcoal-pit black with eerie dim red lanterns glowing out of odd corners and cracks. An Edgar Allan Poe cellar—and there hung his portrait over the apple-bobbing tub, raven-bedecked and with a cracked grin under those dark-pool eyes and that ponderous brow. This was his cellar, to be sure, a Masque-of-the-Red-Death cellar.

And here were the Poe people; miniature versions of his evil creatures: enough hideous beasts to fill page after page, and all shrunk down to child size. Devils galore, with papier-mâché masks, and hooves and tails of red rope, each with a crimson fork on the end; a gaggle of poke-hole ghosts; a mechanical cardboard man; two wolfmen; four vampires with wax teeth; one mummy; one ten-tentacled sea beast; three Frankenstein monsters; one Bride of same; and one monster of indefinite shape and design, something like a jellyfish made of plastic bags.

And Raylee.

Raylee came last; was last to slip silently and trembling through the portal of the yellow front door; was last to slip even more silently down the creaking cellar steps to the Poe cellar below. She came cat-silent and cautious, holding her breath—was indeed dressed cat-like, in whiskered mask, black tights, and black rope tail, all black to mix silently with the black basement.

No one saw her come in; only the black-beetle eyes of Poe over the apple tub noted her arrival.

The apple tub was well in use by now, a host of devils, ghosts, and Frankensteins clamoring around it and eagerly awaiting a turn at its game under Poe's watchful eyes.

"I got one!" shouted one red devil, triumphantly pulling a glossy apple from his mouth; no devil mask here, but a red-painted face, red and dripping from the tub's water. It was Peter, one of the taunting boys in Raylee's class.

Raylee hung back in the shadows.

"I got one!" shouted a Frankenstein monster.

"And me!" from his Bride. Two crisp red apples were held aloft for Poe's inspection.

"And me!" "And me!" shouted Draculas, hunchbacks, little green men.

Spooks and wolfmen shouted too.

One apple left.

"Who hasn't tried yet?" cried Cleo, resplendent in witch's garb. She was a miniature Ms. Grinby. She leaned her broom against the tub, called for attention.

"Who hasn't tried?"

Raylee tried to sink into the shadows' protection but could not. A deeper darkness was what she needed; she was spotted.

"Raylee! Raylee!" shouted Cleo. "Come get your apple!" It was a singsong, as Raylee held her hands out, appleless, and stepped into the circle of ghouls.

She was terrified. She trembled so hard she could not hold her hands still on the side of the metal tub as she leaned over it. She wanted to bolt from the room, up the stairs, and out through the yellow doorway into the dark night.

"Dunk! Dunk!" the ghoul circle began to chant, impatient.

Raylee stared down into the water, saw her dark reflection and Poe's mingled by the ripples of the bobbing apple.

"Dunk! Dunk!" the circle chanted.

Raylee pushed herself from the reflection, stared at the faces surrounding her. "I don't want to!"

"Dunk!..." the chant faded.

Two dozen cool eyes surveyed her behind eyeholes, weighed her dispassionately in the sharp light of peer pressure. There were ghouls behind those ghoulish masks and eyes.

Someone hissed a laugh as the circle tightened around Raylee. Like a battered leaf with its stem caught under a rock in a high wind, she trembled.

Cleo, alone outside the circle, stepped quickly into it to protect her. She held out her hands. "Raylee—" she began soothingly.

The circle tightened still more, undaunted. Above them all, Poe's eyes in the low crimson light seemed to brighten with anticipation.

Desperate, Cleo suddenly said, "Raylee, tell us a story."

A moment of tension, and then a relaxed "Ah" from the circle.

Raylee shivered.

"Yes, tell us a story!"

This from someone in the suffocating circle, a wolf-man, or perhaps a vampire.

"No, please," Raylee begged. Her cat whiskers and cat tail shivered. "I don't want to!"

"Story! Story!" the circle began to chant.

"No, please!"

"Story, story..."

"Tell us the rest of the other story!"

This from Peter in the back of the circle. A low voice, a command.

Another "Ah."

"Yes, tell us!"

Raylee held her hands to her ears. "No!"

"Tell us!"

"No!"

"Tell us now!"

"I thought you were my friends!" Raylee threw her cat-paw hands out at them, her eyes begging.

"Tell us."

A stifled cry escaped Raylee's throat.

Instinctively, the circle widened. They knew she would tell now. They had commanded her. To be one of them, she would do what they told her to do.

Cleo stepped helplessly back into the circle, leaving Raylee under Poe's twisted grin.

Raylee stood alone shivering for a moment. Then, her eyes on the floor, she ceased trembling, became very calm and still. There was a moment of silence. In the dark basement, all that could be heard was the snap of a candle in a far corner and the slapping of water against the lone apple in the tub behind her. When she looked up her eyes were dull, her voice quiet-calm.

She began to speak.

"They took Pumpkin Head away after that, and they put him in a place with crazy people in it. There was screaming all day and night. Someone was always screaming, or hitting his head against the wall, or crying all the time. Pumpkin Head was very lonely, and very scared.

"But Pumpkin Head's parents loved him more than he ever knew. They decided they couldn't let him stay in that place any longer. So they made a plan, a quiet plan.

"One day, when they went to visit him, they dressed him up in a disguise and carried him away. They carried him far away, where no one would ever look for him, all the way across the country. They hid him, and kept him disguised while they tried to find some way to help him. And after a long search, they found a doctor.

"And the doctor did magical things. He worked for two years on Pumpkin Head, on his face and on his body. He cut into Pumpkin Head's face, and changed it. With plastic, he made it into a real face. He changed the rest of Pumpkin Head's head too, and gave him real hair. And he changed Pumpkin Head's body.

"Pumpkin Head's parents paid the doctor a lot of money, and the doctor did the work of a genius.

"He changed Pumpkin Head completely."

Raylee paused, and a light came into her dull eyes. The circle, and Poe above them, waited with indrawn breath.

Waited to say "Ah."

"He changed Pumpkin Head into a little girl."

Breath was pulled back deeper, or let out in little gasps.

The light grew in Raylee's eyes.

"There were things that Pumpkin Head—now not Pumpkin Head anymore—had to do to be a girl. He had to be careful how he dressed, and how he acted. He had to be careful how he talked, and he always had to be calm. He was very frightened of what would happen if he didn't stay calm. For his face was really just a wonderful plastic one. The real Pumpkin Head was still inside, locked in, waiting to come out."

Raylee looked up at them, and her voice suddenly became something different. Hard and rasping.

Her eyes were stoked coals.

"All he ever wanted was friends."

Her cat mask fell away. Her little girl face became soft and bloated and began to grow as if someone were blowing up a balloon inside her. Her hair began to pull into the scalp, forming a circled knot at the top. Creases appeared up and down her face.

With a sickening, rubber-inflated sound, the sound of a melon breaking, Raylee's head burst open to its true shape. Her eyes, ears, and nose became soft orange triangles, her mouth a lazy, grinning crescent. She began to breathe with harsh effort, and her voice became a sharp, wheezing lisp.

"He only wanted friends."

Slowly, with care, Raylee reached down into her costume for what lay hidden there.

She drew it out.

In the black cellar, under Poe's approving glare, there were screams.

"My lunch and dinner," she said, "my dinner and breakfast."

THE CIRCLE

by Lewis Shiner

Lewis Shiner (1950–) was born in Oregon and has lived in Africa as well as much of the southern United States. After earning a B.A. in English, he worked as a construction worker, draftsman, commercial artist, house painter, and musician while perfecting his writing skills.

For six years they'd been meeting on Halloween night here at Walter's cabin, and reading ghost stories to each other. Some of the faces varied from year to year, but Lesley had never missed one of the readings.

She'd come alone this year, and as she parked her Datsun at the edge of the graveled road she couldn't help but think of Rob. She'd brought him to the reading the year before, and that night they'd slept together for the first time. It had been nearly two months now since she'd heard from him, and the thought of him left her wavering between guilt and sadness.

Her shoes crunched on pine needles as she dodged the water droplets dripping from the trees overhead. The night was colder than she had expected, the chill seeping quickly through her light jacket.

She hopped onto the porch of the cabin and rapped on the door. Walter's wife, Susan, answered it. "Come in," she said. "You're the first one."

"It's cold out there," Lesley said.

"Isn't it? Tea's ready. Sit down and I'll bring you a cup."

Lesley had barely settled by the fireplace when the others began to trickle in. Some of them had books, others had manuscripts, most of them also had wine or beer. All of them wrote, several of them professionally, and about half the stories each year had been written for the occasion.

Lesley hadn't felt up to writing one herself this year. In fact she hadn't felt up to much of anything since she and Rob had broken up. His bitterness had hurt her badly, and she was hoping that something would happen tonight to pull her back out of herself.

She hoped it would be the way it used to, when the stories had been chilling and the nights had been damp and eerie, and they'd gotten themselves so scared sometimes that they hadn't gone home until daylight.

They'd been younger then, of course. Now that they were all closing in on thirty they seemed to be more afraid of election results and property taxes than they were of vampires and werewolves.

About nine-thirty Walter stood up and ceremonially lighted the candelabra over the fireplace. The other lamps were turned off, and Walter stood for a moment in the flickering candlelight. He looked a bit like an accountant in his sweater and slacks, with his horn-rimmed glasses and his neatly trimmed mustache.

"Well," he said, clearing his throat, "I think we're all here. Before we get started, we've got something unusual I wanted to tell you about. I got this in the mail last week." He held up a large manila envelope. "It's from Rob Tranchin, in Mexico."

Lesley felt a pang again. "Did he—" she blurted out. "Did he say how he is?"

She felt all the eyes in the room turning on her. The others had never liked Rob all that well, had only put up with him for her sake. While all of them dabbled in the occult, Rob was the only one who had ever taken it seriously, and on more than one occasion he'd had shouted arguments with some of them on the subject.

"I, uh, can't really tell," Walter said. "There was a note inside, but it didn't say much. Just said that he'd written a story for us and that he wanted somebody to read it at tonight's, uh, gathering. It's not very long— I took a quick glance at it—so if nobody minds I'll just draw a card for Rob and one of us can read it when that turn comes around."

Behind Lesley, Brian muttered, "I hope it's not some more of that occult shit of his," but there was no formal objection.

Walter took the ace through eight from a deck of

cards and shuffled them, then let each of the others
draw for a turn. Brian had the ace and read "Heavy
Set" by Bradbury. Walter followed with a new story
that he'd just sold, another Halloween story, and the
chill seemed to creep in through the windows. Lesley
read a piece from Beaumont and even gave herself
shudders.

Then Susan took a turn, her straight blond hair and
pale skin looking cold and waxen in the candles' flicker.
Everyone shifted nervously as she finished, and Lesley
thought happily that it was really happening again.
We've done it, she thought. We've gotten ourselves so
worked up that we're ready to believe anything.

"It's Rob's turn," Walter said quietly. "Anyone want
to do the honors?"

When no one else spoke up, Lesley said, "I will."

I'm still carrying him, she thought as she took the
envelope from Walter. Without wanting to, she finished
the thought: someone has to. Poor childish Rob, with
his tantrums and his grandiose dreams. How long would
he keep haunting them?

She took the manuscript out of the envelope. It was
handwritten on some kind of ragged paper that looked
like parchment. She recognized the scrawled printing,
despite the peculiar brownish ink he'd used.

She glanced at her watch, then went back to the
manuscript. "It's called 'The Circle,'" she said.

She began to read.

"'For six years they'd been meeting on Halloween
night, here at the cabin by the lake, and reading ghost
stories to each other.'"

Lesley looked up. Something about the story was
making her nervous, and she could see that same unease
on the shadowy faces around her.

"'Some of the faces varied from year to year, but a
central group remained the same. They had a lot in
common—they played their games with each other,
went to movies together, and sometimes they went to
bed with each other.'"

Lesley felt a blush starting up her neck. She might
have known he would do something like this to em-

barrass her. He'd been so jealous of the few stories she'd sold, and when she'd tried to offer him some advice he'd blown up. That had been the first quarrel, and he'd come back to it again and again, more bitter each time, until finally he'd left for Mexico.

Well, I'm the one reading this thing, she thought. If it gets any more personal, I'll just stop.

"'Together,'" she read, "'they'd decided that the supernatural was fit material for stories on Halloween, and not much else. Thus they, in their infinite wisdom, were not prepared for what happened to them that Halloween night.

"'The leader of the circle got a story in the mail that week. It was written by someone he had known, but never really considered a friend. Because of his beliefs, he didn't recognize the power that lay in the pages and in the ink that the story was written on. And so he accepted the challenge to read the story aloud that Halloween.

"'They met at the cabin and read their stories, and then they began to read the story by the man who was not with them anymore. And as soon as they began to read it, a heavy mist settled down around the cabin.

"'It was like a fog, but so thick you could almost feel it, squeeze between your fingers. It carried the salt smell of an ocean that shouldn't have been there, and everywhere it touched, the world ceased to exist.'"

Lesley's mouth had gone dry. She was leaning forward to pick up her teacup when she saw the window.

"Oh my God..." she whispered.

Beyond the window was a solid mass of white.

They all stared at the fog outside the window. Guy and his new girl friend Dana had been sitting under the window, and they'd moved into the center of the room. "What is it?" Dana asked. Her voice had a tremor in it that made Lesley even more frightened than before.

"It's called fog," Brian sneered. "Haven't you ever seen fog before?" He started for the door. "Look, I'll show it to you."

"Don't—" Lesley started, but her throat caught before she could finish the sentence.

The candlelight glinted off Brian's moist lips and oily hair. "What's the matter with you guys? What are you afraid of?"

He jerked the door open.

The fog lay outside like a wall of cotton wool. The edge of it, where the door had been, was as smooth as if it had been cut with a razor. Not even the thinnest wisp tried to reach through the doorway.

"See?" Brian said, sticking his arm into it. "Fog." Lesley saw his nose wrinkle, and then she smelled it herself. It was a salty, low-tide odor like dead fish.

"Yuck," Brian said. He took a step toward the porch of the cabin, lost his balance, and caught himself by gripping the molding on either side of the door. "What the hell—?"

He extended one leg as far as it would go, then lay down and reached out into the fog. "There's nothing there."

"I don't like this," Susan said, but no one was listening to her.

"No porch," Brian said, "no ground, nothing."

Almost imperceptibly they all began to move closer to the fireplace.

"Close the door," Walter said calmly, and Brian did as he was told. "Lesley, what's the next line of the story?"

"'With the fog came the sound of the wind. It howled and it screamed, but the air never moved and the fog lay heavy over the cabin.'"

The noise began.

It started as a low whistle, then built into a moaning, shrieking crescendo. It sounded less like a wind than a chorus of human voices, frightened and tortured out of their minds.

"Stop it!" Susan screamed. "Stop it, please make it stop!" Walter put his arms around her and held her head to his chest. She began to sob quietly.

They were now a circle in fact, a tight circle on the floor in front of the fireplace, knees touching, eyes searching each other's faces for some sign of understanding.

"What is it?" Dana cried. She was nearly shouting in order to be heard. "Where's it coming from?"

Lesley and Walter looked at each other, then Lesley's gaze dropped to the floor.

"It's that story, isn't it?" Dana said, her voice so high it was starting to crack. "Isn't it?"

"It must be," Walter said. His voice was so low that Lesley could barely hear it over the howling outside. "Rob must have found something in Mexico. A way to get back at us."

"This isn't happening," Brian said. "It's not. It can't be."

"It is," Walter said, raising his voice over the wind. "Pretending it isn't real is not going to help." Susan whimpered, and he held her tighter to his chest. "Look, we've all read stories like this. Some of us have written them. We all get irritated when people refuse to accept what's happening to them. How long is it going to take for us to admit what's happening here?"

"All right," Brian said. "It's real. What do we do?"

Lesley said, "The paper and ink. Rob said they were special. In the story."

"Why don't we just burn the damned thing?" Brian said. "We should have done that in the first place." As if in answer, the wind roared up to a deafening volume.

"No," said Walter. He waited until the noise subsided again and added, "What if we burn it and trap ourselves here? If only we knew how it ends."

"That's easy enough," Brian said. He reached across and took the papers from Lesley's unresisting fingers.

"No!" Walter shouted, lunging at him, but Brian had already flipped over to the last page.

"We all die," he said, handing the story back to Lesley. "Not very well written, but pretty gruesome." His levity failed completely. The wind was so loud it seemed to Lesley that the walls should have been shaken to pieces.

"Ideas?" Walter said. "Anybody?"

"I say burn it," Brian said again. "What can happen?"

"Rewrite it," Lesley said.

"What?" Walter asked. Lesley realized that the awful noise had swallowed her words.

"Rewrite it!" she repeated. "Change the ending!"

"I like it," Walter said. "Guy?"

He shrugged. "Worth a try. Anybody got a pen?"

"No," Lesley said. "I don't think that'll work."

"Why not?"

"I think," she said, "it's written in blood."

She knew it was up to her. It was like belling the cat—her idea, her responsibility. Before any of the others could stop her, she got a safety pin out of her purse and jabbed it into the index finger of her left hand.

She rolled the point of the pin in the droplet of blood, then tried to draw an X across the bottom of the page she'd been reading from. The point of the pin just wouldn't hold enough. Finally she just wiped her finger across it, and then did the same thing on the last two pages.

"Now," she said. "What do I write?"

They all sat and looked at each other while the ghost wind shrieked at them.

"How about, 'Everything returned to normal'?" Guy said.

"What's normal?" Brian asked.

"He's got a point," Walter admitted. "We may need to be more specific."

"Not too specific," Lesley said. "I've only got so much blood."

No one laughed.

"Okay," Walter said. "Does anybody know what time Lesley started reading?"

"I checked," Lesley said. "It was eleven-eighteen."

"All right. How about, 'Everything returned to the way it had been at eleven-eighteen that night'?"

There were nods all around. "Go for it," Guy said.

This time Lesley had to use the pin. It was slow going, but she finally got the words scrawled across the bottom of the page.

The wind continued to scream.

"Read it," Walter said.

Lesley's hands were shaking. Come on, she told herself, you didn't lose that much blood. But she knew it wasn't that. What if she read it and it didn't work? She couldn't stand that horrible, shrill noise much longer.

From the back of her mind a grim thought began to

nag at her. What were the gruesome things the story said happened to them?

Let it work, she prayed. Let everything be the way it had been. Just exactly the way it had been.

"'Everything,'" she read, her shaking voice barely topping the roar of the wind, "'returned to the way it had been at eleven-eighteen that night.'"

It was quiet.

The night was clear and cold, and water dripped from the trees to the layer of pine needles on the ground.

Lesley looked at her watch. It was 11:18.

"It's called 'The Circle,'" she said.

She began to read.

ALL SOULS'

by Edith Wharton

*Edith Wharton (1862–1937) was born Edith Newbold,
in New York. She was educated at home by tutors and
governesses, and almost died of typhoid at the age of
nine. From that time on, she was haunted by fears of
the supernatural and eventually began to write on the
subject. In 1885 she married Edward Wharton, with
whom she lived in France for most of her life. Her writing
was most influenced and encouraged by her friend Henry
James, who shared her predilections.*

*Ethan Frome (1911) is probably the best known of
her forty-seven books. Many honors came her way including the Gold Medal, membership in the National
Institute of Arts and Letters, a Pulitzer Prize, and the
rank of Officer in the Legion of Honor.*

Queer and inexplicable as the business was, on the surface it appeared fairly simple—at the time, at least;
but with the passing of years, and owing to there not
having been a single witness of what happened except
Sara Clayburn herself, the stories about it have become
so exaggerated, and often so ridiculously inaccurate,
that it seems necessary that someone connected with
the affair, though not actually present—I repeat that
when it happened my cousin was (or thought she was)
quite alone in her house—should record the few facts
actually known.

In those days I was often at Whitegates (as the place
had always been called)—I was there, in fact, not long
before, and almost immediately after, the strange happenings of those thirty-six hours. Jim Clayburn and his
widow were both my cousins, and because of that, and
of my intimacy with them, both families think I am
more likely than anybody else to be able to get at the

facts, as far as they can be called facts, and as anybody
can get at them. So I have written down, as clearly as
I could, the gist of the various talks I had with cousin
Sara, when she could be got to talk—it wasn't often—
about what occurred during that mysterious weekend.

I read the other day in a book by a fashionable es-
sayist that ghosts went out when electric light came
in. What nonsense! The writer, though he is fond of
dabbling, in a literary way, in the supernatural, hasn't
even reached the threshold of his subject. As between
turreted castles patrolled by headless victims with
clanking chains, and the comfortable suburban house
with a refrigerator and central heating where you feel,
as soon as you're in it, *that there's something wrong*,
give me the latter for sending a chill down the spine!
And, by the way, haven't you noticed that it's generally
not the high-strung and imaginative who see ghosts,
but the calm matter-of-fact people who don't believe in
them, and are sure they wouldn't mind if they did see
one? Well, that was the case with Sara Clayburn and
her house. The house, in spite of its age—it was built,
I believe, about 1780—was open, airy, high-ceilinged,
with electricity, central heating, and all the modern
appliances: and its mistress was—well, very much like
her house. And, anyhow, this isn't exactly a ghost story
and I've dragged in the analogy only as a way of showing you what kind of woman my cousin was, and how
unlikely it would have seemed that what happened at
Whitegates should have happened just there—or to her.

When Jim Clayburn died the family all thought that,
as the couple had no children, his widow would give up
Whitegates and move either to New York or Boston—
for being of good Colonial stock, with many relatives
and friends, she would have found a place ready for her
in either. But Sara Clayburn seldom did what other
people expected, and in this case she did exactly the
contrary; she stayed at Whitegates.

"What, turn my back on the old house—tear up all
the family roots, and go and hang myself up in a bird-
cage flat in one of those new skyscrapers in Lexington
Avenue, with a bunch of chickweed and a cuttlefish to
replace my good Connecticut mutton? No, thank you.

Here I belong, and here I stay till my executors hand
the place over to Jim's next-of-kin—that stupid fat
Presley boy.... Well, don't let's talk about him. But I
tell you what—I'll keep him out of here as long as I
can." And she did—for being still in the early fifties
when her husband died, and a muscular, resolute figure
of a woman, she was more than a match for the fat
Presley boy, and attended his funeral a few years ago,
in correct mourning, with a faint smile under her veil.

Whitegates was a pleasant hospitable-looking house,
on a height overlooking the stately windings of the
Connecticut River; but it was five or six miles from
Norrington, the nearest town, and its situation would
certainly have seemed remote and lonely to modern
servants. Luckily, however, Sara Clayburn had inherited from her mother-in-law two or three old standbys
who seemed as much a part of the family tradition as
the roof they lived under; and I never heard of her
having any trouble in her domestic arrangements.

The house, in Colonial days, had been foursquare,
with four spacious rooms on the ground floor, an oak-
floored hall dividing them, the usual kitchen extension
at the back, and a good attic under the roof. But Jim's
grandparents, when interest in the "Colonial" began to
revive, in the early eighties, had added two wings, at
right angles to the south front, so that the old "circle"
before the front door became a grassy court, enclosed
on three sides, with a big elm in the middle. Thus the
house was turned into a roomy dwelling, in which the
last three generations of Clayburns had exercised a
large hospitality; but the architect had respected the
character of the old house, and the enlargement made
it more comfortable without lessening its simplicity.
There was a lot of land about it, and Jim Clayburn,
like his fathers before him, farmed it, not without profit,
and played a considerable and respected part in state
politics. The Clayburns were always spoken of as a "good
influence" in the county, and the townspeople were glad
when they learned that Sara did not mean to desert the
place—"though it must be lonesome, winters, living all
alone up there atop of that hill," they remarked as the
days shortened, and the first snow began to pile up
under the quadruple row of elms along the common.

Well, if I've given you a sufficiently clear idea of Whitegates and the Clayburns—who shared with their old house a sort of reassuring orderliness and dignity—I'll efface myself, and tell the tale, not in my cousin's words, for they were too confused and fragmentary, but as I built it up gradually out of her half-avowals and nervous reticences. If the thing happened at all—and I must leave you to judge of that—I think it must have happened in this way...

I

The morning had been bitter, with a driving sleet—though it was only the last day of October—but after lunch a watery sun showed for a while through banked-up woolly clouds, and tempted Sara Clayburn out. She was an energetic walker, and given, at that season, to tramping three or four miles along the valley road, and coming back by way of Shaker's wood. She had made her usual round, and was following the main drive to the house when she overtook a plainly dressed woman walking in the same direction. If the scene had not been so lonely—the way to Whitegates at the end of an autumn day was not a frequented one—Mrs. Clayburn might not have paid any attention to the woman, for she was in no way noticeable; but when she caught up with the intruder, my cousin was surprised to find that she was a stranger—for the mistress of Whitegates prided herself on knowing, at least by sight, most of her country neighbors. It was almost dark, and the woman's face was hardly visible, but Mrs. Clayburn told me she recalled her as middle-aged, plain and rather pale.

Mrs. Clayburn greeted her, and then added: "You're going to the house?"

"Yes, ma'am," the woman answered, in a voice that the Connecticut Valley in old days would have called "foreign," but that would have been unnoticed by ears used to the modern multiplicity of tongues. "No, I couldn't say where she came from," Sara always said. "What struck me as queer was that I didn't know her."

She asked the woman, politely, what she wanted,

and the woman answered: "Only to see one of the girls."
The answer was natural enough, and Mrs. Clayburn
nodded and turned off from the drive to the lower part
of the gardens, so that she saw no more of the visitor
then or afterward. And, in fact, a half hour later something happened which put the stranger entirely out of
her mind. The brisk and light-footed Mrs. Clayburn, as
she approached the house, slipped on a frozen puddle,
turned her ankle and lay suddenly helpless.

Price, the butler, and Agnes, the dour old Scottish
maid whom Sara had inherited from her mother-in-law,
of course knew exactly what to do. In no time they had
their mistress stretched out on a lounge, and Dr. Selgrove had been called up from Norrington. When he
arrived, he ordered Mrs. Clayburn to bed, did the necessary examining and bandaging, and shook his head
over her ankle, which he feared was fractured. He
thought, however, that if she would swear not to get
up, or even shift the position of her leg, he could spare
her the discomfort of putting it in plaster. Mrs. Clayburn agreed, the more promptly as the doctor warned
her that any rash movement would prolong her immobility. Her quick imperious nature made the prospect trying, and she was annoyed with herself for having
been so clumsy. But the mischief was done, and she
immediately thought what an opportunity she would
have for going over her accounts and catching up with
her correspondence. So she settled down resignedly in
her bed.

"And you won't miss much, you know, if you have
to stay there a few days. It's beginning to snow, and it
looks as if we were in for a good spell of it," the doctor
remarked, glancing through the window as he gathered
up his implements. "Well, we don't often get snow here
as early as this; but winter's got to begin sometime,"
he concluded philosophically. At the door he stopped to
add: "You don't want me to send up a nurse from Norrington? Not to nurse you, you know; there's nothing
much to do till I see you again. But this is a pretty
lonely place when the snow begins, and I thought
maybe—"

Sara Clayburn laughed. "Lonely? With my old serv-

ants? You forget how many winters I've spent here alone
with them. Two of them were with me in my mother-
in-law's time."

"That's so," Dr. Selgrove agreed. "You're a good deal
luckier than most people, that way. Well, let me see;
this is Saturday. We'll have to let the inflammation go
down before we can X-ray you. Monday morning, first
thing, I'll be here with the X-ray man. If you want me
sooner, call me up." And he was gone.

II

The foot at first had not been very painful; but toward
the small hours Mrs. Clayburn began to suffer. She was
a bad patient, like most healthy and active people. Not
being used to pain, she did not know how to bear it,
and the hours of wakefulness and immobility seemed
endless. Agnes, before leaving her, had made everything as comfortable as possible. She had put a jug of
lemonade within reach, and had even (Mrs. Clayburn
thought it odd afterward) insisted on bringing in a tray
with sandwiches and a thermos of tea. "If case you're
hungry in the night, madam."

"Thank you; but I'm never hungry in the night. And
I certainly shan't be tonight—only thirsty. I think I'm
feverish."

"Well, there's the lemonade, madam."

"That will do. Take the other things away, please."
(Sara had always hated the sight of unwanted food
"messing about" in her room.)

"Very well, madam. Only you might—"

"Please take it away," Mrs. Clayburn repeated ir-
ritably.

"Very good, madam." But as Agnes went out, her
mistress heard her set the tray down softly on a table
behind the screen which shut off the door.

Obstinate old goose! she thought, rather touched by
the old woman's insistence.

Sleep, once it had gone, would not return, and the
long black hours moved more and more slowly. How
late the dawn came in November! "If only I could move
my leg," she grumbled.

She lay still and strained her ears for the first steps of the servants. Whitegates was an early house, its mistress setting the example; it would surely not be long now before one of the women came. She was tempted to ring for Agnes, but refrained. The woman had been up late, and this was Sunday morning, when the household was always allowed a little extra time. Mrs. Clayburn reflected restlessly: "I was a fool not to let her leave the tea beside the bed, as she wanted to. I wonder if I could get up and get it?" But she remembered the doctor's warning, and dared not move. Anything rather than risk prolonging her imprisonment....

Ah, there was the stable clock striking. How loud it sounded in the snowy stillness! One—two—three—four—five...

What? Only five? Three hours and a quarter more before she could hope to hear the door handle turned. ...After a while she dozed off again, uncomfortably.

Another sound aroused her. Again the stable clock. She listened. But the room was still in deep darkness, and only six strokes fell.... She thought of reciting something to put her to sleep; but she seldom read poetry, and being naturally a good sleeper, she could not remember any of the usual devices against insomnia. The whole of her leg felt like lead now. The bandages had grown terribly tight—her ankle must have swollen.... She lay staring at the dark windows, watching for the first glimmer of dawn. At last she saw a pale filter of daylight through the shutters. One by one the objects between the bed and the window recovered first their outline, then their bulk, and seemed to be stealthily regrouping themselves, after goodness knows what secret displacements during the night. Who that has lived in an old house could possibly believe that the furniture in it stays still all night? Mrs. Clayburn almost fancied she saw one little slender-legged table slipping hastily back into its place.

It knows Agnes is coming, and it's afraid, she thought whimsically. Her bad night must have made her imaginative, for such nonsense as that about the furniture had never occurred to her before....

At length, after hours more, as it seemed, the stable

clock struck eight. Only another quarter of an hour.
She watched the hand moving slowly across the face of
the little clock beside her bed...ten minutes...five...
only five! Agnes was as punctual as destiny...in two
minutes now she would come. The two minutes passed,
and she did not come. Poor Agnes—she had looked pale
and tired the night before. She had overslept herself,
no doubt—or perhaps she felt ill, and would send the
housemaid to replace her. Mrs. Clayburn waited.

She waited half an hour; then she reached up to the
bell at the head of the bed. Poor old Agnes—her mistress felt guilty about waking her. But Agnes did not
appear—and after a considerable interval Mrs. Clayburn, now with a certain impatience, rang again. She
rang once; twice; three times—but still no one came.

Once more she waited; then she said to herself: "There
must be something wrong with the electricity." Well—
she could find out by switching on the bed lamp at her
elbow (how admirably the room was equipped with every
practical appliance!). She switched it on—but no light
came. Electric current cut off; and it was Sunday, and
nothing could be done about it till the next morning.
Unless it turned out to be just a burnt-out fuse, which
Price could remedy. Well, in a moment now someone
would surely come to her door.

It was nine o'clock before she admitted to herself that
something uncommonly strange must have happened
in the house. She began to feel a nervous apprehension;
but she was not the woman to encourage it. If only she
had had the telephone put in her room, instead of out
on the landing! She measured mentally the distance to
be traveled, remembered Dr. Selgrove's admonition, and
wondered if her broken ankle would carry her there.
She dreaded the prospect of being put in plaster, but
she had to get to the telephone, whatever happened.

She wrapped herself in her dressing gown, found a
walking stick, and, resting heavily on it, dragged herself to the door. In her bedroom the careful Agnes had
closed and fastened the shutters, so that it was not
much lighter there than at dawn; but outside in the
corridor the cold whiteness of the snowy morning seemed
almost reassuring. Mysterious things—dreadful
things—were associated with darkness; and here was

the wholesome prosaic daylight come again to banish
them. Mrs. Clayburn looked about her and listened.
Silence. A deep nocturnal silence in that day-lit house,
in which five people were presumably coming and going
about their work. It was certainly strange....She looked
out the window, hoping to see someone crossing the
court or coming along the drive. But no one was in sight,
and the snow seemed to have the place to itself: a quiet
steady snow. It was still falling, with a businesslike
regularity, muffling the outer world in layers on layers
of thick white velvet, and intensifying the silence within.
A noiseless world—were people so sure that absence
of noise was what they wanted? Let them first try a
lonely country house in a November snowstorm!

She dragged herself along the passage to the telephone. When she unhooked the receiver she noticed
that her hand trembled.

She rang up the pantry—no answer. She rang again.
Silence—more silence! It seemed to be piling itself up
like the snow on the roof and in the gutters. Silence.
How many people that she knew had any idea what
silence was—and how loud it sounded when you really
listened to it?

Again she waited: then she rang up "Central." No
answer. She tried three times. After that she tried the
pantry again....The telephone was cut off, then; like
the electric current. Who was at work downstairs, iso-
lating her thus from the world? Her heart began to
hammer. Luckily there was a chair near the telephone,
and she sat down to recover her strength—or was it
her courage?

Agnes and the housemaid slept in the nearest wing.
She would certainly get as far as that when she had
pulled herself together. Had she the courage—? Yes,
of course she had. She had always been regarded as a
plucky woman; and had so regarded herself. But this
silence—

It occurred to her that by looking from the window
of a neighboring bathroom she could see the kitchen
chimney. There ought to be smoke coming from it at
that hour; and if there were she thought she would be
less afraid to go on. She got as far as the bathroom and

looking through the window saw that no smoke came from the chimney. Her sense of loneliness grew more acute. Whatever had happened belowstairs must have happened before the morning's work had begun. The cook had not had time to light the fire, the other servants had not yet begun their round. She sank down on the nearest chair, struggling against her fears. What next would she discover if she carried on her investigations?

The pain in her ankle made progress difficult; but she was aware of it now only as an obstacle to haste. No matter what it cost her in physical suffering, she must find out what was happening belowstairs—or had happened. But first she would go to the maid's room. And if that were empty—well, somehow she would have to get herself downstairs.

She limped along the passage, and on the way steadied herself by resting her hand on a radiator. It was stone-cold. Yet, in that well-ordered house in winter the central heating, though damped down at night, was never allowed to go out, and by eight in the morning a mellow warmth pervaded the rooms. The icy chill of the pipes startled her. It was the chauffeur who looked after the heating—so he too was involved in the mystery, whatever it was, as well as the house servants. But this only deepened the problem.

III

At Agnes's door Mrs. Clayburn paused and knocked. She expected no answer, and there was none. She opened the door and went in. The room was dark and very cold. She went to the window and flung back the shutters; then she looked slowly around, vaguely apprehensive of what she might see. The room was empty but what frightened her was not so much its emptiness as its air of scrupulous and undisturbed order. There was no sign of anyone having lately dressed in it—or undressed the night before. And the bed had not been slept in.

Mrs. Clayburn leaned against the wall for a moment; then she crossed the floor and opened the cupboard. That was where Agnes kept her dresses; and the dresses were there, neatly hanging in a row. On the shelf above were Agnes's few and unfashionable hats, rearrangements of her mistress's old ones. Mrs. Clayburn, who knew them all, looked at the shelf, and saw that one was missing. And so was the warm winter coat she had given to Agnes the previous winter.

The woman was out, then; had gone out, no doubt, the night before, since the bed was unslept in, the dressing and washing appliances untouched. Agnes, who never set foot out of the house after dark, who despised the movies as much as she did the wireless, and could never be persuaded that a little innocent amusement was a necessary element in life, had deserted the house on a snowy winter night, while her mistress lay upstairs, suffering and helpless! Why had she gone, and where had she gone? When she was undressing Mrs. Clayburn the night before, taking her orders, trying to make her more comfortable, was she already planning this mysterious nocturnal escape? Or had something— the mysterious and dreadful Something for the clue of which Mrs. Clayburn was still groping—occurred later in the evening, sending the maid downstairs and out of doors into the bitter night? Perhaps one of the men at the garage—where the chauffeur and gardener lived—had been suddenly taken ill, and someone had run up to the house for Agnes. Yes—that must be the explanation.... Yet how much it left unexplained.

Next to Agnes's room was the linen room; beyond that was the housemaid's door. Mrs. Clayburn went to it and knocked. "Mary!" No one answered, and she went in. The room was in the same immaculate order as her maid's, and here too the bed was unslept in, and there were no signs of dressing or undressing. The two women had no doubt gone out together—gone where?

More and more the cold unanswering silence of the house weighed down on Mrs. Clayburn. She had never thought of it as a big house, but now, in this snowy winter light, it seemed immense, and full of ominous corners around which one dared not to look.

Beyond the housemaid's room were the back stairs.

It was the nearest way down, and every step that Mrs. Clayburn took was increasingly painful; but she decided to walk slowly back, the whole length of the passage, and go down by the front stairs. She did not know why she did this; but she felt that at the moment she was past reasoning, and had better obey her instinct.

More than once she had explored the ground floor alone in the small hours, in search of unwonted midnight noises; but now it was not the idea of noises that frightened her, but that inexorable and hostile silence, the sense that the house had retained in full daylight its nocturnal mystery, and was watching her as she was watching it; that in entering those empty orderly rooms she might be disturbing some unseen confabulation on which beings of flesh-and-blood had better not intrude.

The broad oak stairs were beautifully polished, and so slippery that she had to cling to the rail and let herself down tread by tread. And as she descended, the silence descended with her—heavier, denser, more absolute. She seemed to feel its steps just behind her, softly keeping time with hers. It had a quality she had never been aware of in any other silence, as though it were not merely an absence of sound, a thin barrier between the ear and the surging murmur of life just beyond, but an impenetrable substance made out of the worldwide cessation of all life and all movement.

Yes, that was what laid a chill on her: the feeling that there was no limit to this silence, no outer margin, nothing beyond it. By this time she had reached the foot of the stairs and was limping across the hall to the drawing room. Whatever she found there, she was sure, would be mute and lifeless; but what would it be? The bodies of her dead servants, mown down by some homicidal maniac? And what if it were her turn next—if he were waiting for her behind the heavy curtains of the room she was about to enter? Well, she must find out—she must face whatever lay in wait. Not impelled by bravery—the last drop of courage had oozed out of her—but because anything, anything was better than to remain shut up in that snowbound house without knowing whether she was alone in it or not, "I must

find that out, I must find that out," she repeated to
herself in a sort of meaningless singsong.

The cold outer light flooded the drawing room. The
shutters had not been closed, nor the curtains drawn.
She looked about her. The room was empty, and every
chair in its usual place. Her armchair was pushed up
by the chimney, and the cold hearth was piled with the
ashes of the fire at which she had warmed herself before
starting on her ill-fated walk. Even her empty coffee
cup stood on a table near the armchair. It was evident
that the servants had not been in the room since she
had left it the day before after luncheon. And suddenly
the conviction entered into her that, as she found the
drawing room, so she would find the rest of the house;
cold, orderly—and empty. She would find nothing, she
would find no one. She no longer felt any dread of or-
dinary human dangers lurking in those dumb spaces
ahead of her. She knew she was utterly alone under
her own roof. She sat down to rest her aching ankle,
and looked slowly about her.

There were the other rooms to be visited, and she
was determined to go through them all—but she knew
in advance that they would give no answer to her question. She knew it, seemingly, from the quality of the
silence which enveloped her. There was no break, no
thinnest crack in it anywhere. It had the cold continuity
of the snow which was still falling steadily outside.

She had no idea how long she waited before nerving
herself to continue her inspection. She no longer felt
the pain in her ankle, but was only conscious that she
must not bear her weight on it, and therefore moved
very slowly, supporting herself on each piece of furniture in her path. On the ground floor no shutter had
been closed, no curtain drawn, and she progressed without difficulty from room to room: the library, her morning room, the dining room. In each of them, every piece
of furniture was in its usual place. In the dining room,
the table had been laid for her dinner of the previous
evening, and the candelabra, with candles unlit, stood
reflected in the dark mahogany. She was not the kind
of woman to nibble a poached egg on a tray when she
was alone, but always came down to the dining room,
and had what she called a civilized meal.

The back premises remained to be visited. From the dining room she entered the pantry, and there too everything was in irreproachable order. She opened the door and looked down the back passage with its neat linoleum floor covering. The deep silence accompanied her; she still felt it moving watchfully at her side, as though she were its prisoner and it might throw itself upon her if she attempted to escape. She limped on toward the kitchen. That of course would be empty too, and immaculate. But she must see it.

She leaned a minute in the embrasure of a window in the passage. It's like the "Mary Celeste"—a "Mary Celeste" on *terra firma,* she thought, recalling the unsolved sea mystery of her childhood. No one ever knew what happened on board the "Mary Celeste." And perhaps no one will ever know what has happened here. Even I shan't know.

At the thought, her latent fear seemed to take on a new quality. It was like an icy liquid running through every vein, and lying in a pool about her heart. She understood now that she had never before known what fear was, and that most of the people she had met had probably never known either. For this sensation was something quite different....

It absorbed her so completely that she was not aware how long she remained leaning there. But suddenly a new impulse pushed her forward, and she walked on toward the scullery. She went there first because there was a service slide in the wall, through which she might peep into the kitchen without being seen; and some indefinable instinct told her that the kitchen held the clue to the mystery. She still felt strongly that whatever had happened in the house must have its source and center in the kitchen.

In the scullery, as she had expected, everything was clean and tidy. Whatever had happened, no one in the house appeared to have been taken by surprise; there was nowhere any sign of confusion or disorder. It looks as if they'd known beforehand, and put everything straight, she thought. She glanced at the wall facing the door, and saw that the slide was open. And then, as she was approaching it, the silence was broken. A

voice was speaking in the kitchen—a man's voice, low
but emphatic, and which she had never heard before.

She stood still, cold with fear. But this fear was again
a different one. Her previous terrors had been specu-
lative, conjectural, a ghostly emanation of the surrounding silence. This was a plain everyday dread of
evildoers. Oh, God, why had she not remembered her
husband's revolver, which ever since his death had lain
in a drawer in her room?

She turned to retreat across the smooth slippery floor
but halfway her stick slipped from her, and crashed
down on the tiles. The noise seemed to echo on and on
through the emptiness, and she stood still, aghast. Now
that she had betrayed her presence, flight was useless.
Whoever was beyond the kitchen door would be upon
her in a second. . . .

But to her astonishment the voice went on speaking.
It was as though neither the speaker nor his listeners
had heard her. The invisible stranger spoke so low that
she could not make out what he was saying, but the
tone was passionately earnest, almost threatening. The
next moment she realized that he was speaking in a
foreign language, a language unknown to her. Once
more her terror was surmounted by the urgent desire
to know what was going on, so close to her yet unseen.
She crept to the slide, peered cautiously through into
the kitchen, and saw that it was as orderly and empty
as the other rooms. But in the middle of the carefully
scoured table stood a portable wireless, and the voice
she heard came out of it. . . .

She must have fainted then, she supposed; at any
rate she felt so weak and dizzy that her memory of what
next happened remained indistinct. But in the course
of time she groped her way back to the pantry, and
there found a bottle of spirits—brandy or whiskey, she
could not remember which. She found a glass, poured
herself a stiff drink, and while it was flushing through
her veins, managed—she never knew with how many
shuddering delays—to drag herself through the deserted ground floor, up the stairs, and down the corridor
to her own room. There, apparently, she fell across the
threshold, again unconscious. . . .

When she came to, she remembered, her first care

had been to lock herself in; then to recover her husband's revolver. It was not loaded, but she found some cartridges, and succeeded in loading it. Then she remembered that Agnes, on leaving her the evening before, had refused to carry away the tray with the tea and sandwiches, and she fell on them with a sudden hunger. She recalled also noticing that a flask of brandy had been put beside the thermos, and being vaguely surprised. Agnes's departure, then, had been deliberately planned, and she had known that her mistress, who never touched spirits, might have need of a stimulant before she returned. Mrs. Clayburn poured some of the brandy into her tea, and swallowed it greedily.

After that (she told me later) she remembered that she had managed to start a fire in her grate, and after warming herself, had got back into her bed, piling on it all the coverings she could find. The afternoon passed in a haze of pain, out of which there emerged now and then a dim shape of fear—the fear that she might lie there alone and untended till she died of cold, and of the terror of her solitude. For she was sure by this time that the house was empty—completely empty, from garret to cellar. She knew it was so, she could not tell why; but again she felt that it must be because of the peculiar quality of the silence—the silence which had dogged her steps wherever she went, and was now folded down on her like a pall. She was sure that the nearness of any other human being, however dumb and secret, would have made a faint crack in the texture of that silence, flawed it as a sheet of glass is flawed by a pebble thrown against it....

IV

"Is that easier?" the doctor asked, lifting himself from bending over her ankle. He shook his head disapprovingly. "Looks to me as if you'd disobeyed orders—eh? Been moving about, haven't you? And I guess Dr. Selgrove told you to keep quiet till he saw you again, didn't he?"

The speaker was a stranger, whom Mrs. Clayburn knew only by name. Her own doctor had been called away that morning to the bedside of an old patient in Baltimore, and had asked this young man, who was beginning to be known at Norrington, to replace him. The newcomer was shy, and somewhat familiar, as the shy often are, and Mrs. Clayburn decided that she did not much like him. But before she could convey this by the tone of her reply (and she was past mistress of the shades of disapproval) she heard Agnes speaking—yes, Agnes, the same, the usual Agnes, standing behind the doctor, neat and stern-looking as ever. "Mrs. Clayburn must have got up and walked about in the night instead of ringing for me, as she't ought to," Agnes intervened severely.

This was too much! In spite of the pain, which was now exquisite, Mrs. Clayburn laughed. "Ringing for you? How could I, with the electricity cut off?"

"The electricity cut off?" Agnes's surprise was masterly. "Why, when was it cut off?" She pressed her finger on the bell beside the bed, and the call tinkled through the quiet room. "I tried that bell before I left you last night, madam, because if there'd been anything wrong with it I'd have come and slept in the dressing room sooner than leave you here alone."

Mrs. Clayburn lay speechless, staring up at her. "Last night? But last night I was all alone in the house."

Agnes's firm features did not alter. She folded her hands resignedly across her trim apron. "Perhaps the pain's made you a little confused, madam." She looked at the doctor, who nodded.

"The pain in your foot must have been pretty bad," he said.

"It was," Mrs. Clayburn replied. "But it was nothing to the horror of being left alone in this empty house since the day before yesterday, with the heat and the electricity cut off, and the telephone not working."

The doctor was looking at her in evident wonder. Agnes's sallow face flushed slightly, but only as if in indignation at an unjust charge. "But, madam, I made up your fire with my own hands last night—and look, it's smoldering still. I was getting ready to start it again just now, when the doctor came."

"That's so. She was down on her knees before it," the doctor corroborated.

Again Mrs. Clayburn laughed. Ingeniously as the tissue of lies was being woven about her, she felt she could still break through it. "I made up the fire myself yesterday—there was no one else to do it," she said, addressing the doctor, but keeping her eyes on her maid. "I got up twice to put on more coal, because the house was like a sepulcher. The central heating must have been out since Saturday afternoon."

At this incredible statement Agnes's face expressed only a polite distress; but the new doctor was evidently embarrassed at being drawn into an unintelligible controversy with which he had no time to deal. He said he had brought the X-ray photographer with him, but that the ankle was too much swollen to be photographed at present. He asked Mrs. Clayburn to excuse his haste, as he had all Dr. Selgrove's patients to visit besides his own, and promised to come back that evening to decide whether she could be X-rayed then, and whether, as he evidently feared, the ankle would have to be put in plaster. Then, handing his prescriptions to Agnes, he departed.

Mrs. Clayburn spent a feverish and suffering day. She did not feel well enough to carry on the discussion with Agnes; she did not ask to see the other servants. She grew drowsy, and understood that her mind was confused with fever. Agnes and the housemaid waited on her as attentively as usual, and by the time the doctor returned in the evening her temperature had fallen; but she decided not to speak of what was on her mind until Dr. Selgrove reappeared. He was to be back the following evening; and the new doctor preferred to wait for him before deciding to put the ankle in plaster—though he feared this was now inevitable.

V

That afternoon Mrs. Clayburn had me summoned by telephone, and I arrived at Whitegates the following day. My cousin, who looked pale and nervous, merely pointed to her foot, which had been put in plaster, and thanked me for coming to keep her company. She explained that Dr. Selgrove had been taken suddenly ill in Baltimore, and would not be back for several days, but that the young man who replaced him seemed fairly competent. She made no allusion to the strange incidents I have set down, but I felt at once that she had received a shock which her accident, however painful, could not explain.

Finally, one evening, she told me the story of her strange weekend, as it had presented itself to her unusually clear and accurate mind, and as I have recorded it above. She did not tell me this till several weeks after my arrival; but she was still upstairs at the time, and obliged to divide her days between her bed and a lounge. During those endless intervening weeks, she told me, she had thought the whole matter over: and though the events of the mysterious thirty-six hours were still vivid to her, they had already lost something of their haunting terror, and she had finally decided not to reopen the question with Agnes, or to touch on it in speaking to the other servants. Dr. Selgrove's illness had been not only serious but prolonged. He had not yet returned, and it was reported that as soon as he was well enough he would go on a West Indian cruise, and not resume his practice at Norrington till the spring. Dr. Selgrove, as my cousin was perfectly aware, was the only person who could prove that thirty-six hours had elapsed between his visit and that of his successor; and the latter, a shy young man, burdened by the heavy additional practice suddenly thrown on his shoulders, told me (when I risked a little private talk with him) that in the haste of Dr. Selgrove's departure the only instructions he had given about Mrs. Clayburn were summed up in the brief memorandum: "Broken ankle. Have X-rayed."

Knowing my cousin's authoritative character, I was surprised at her decision not to speak to the servants of what had happened; but on thinking it over I concluded she was right. They were all exactly as they had been before that unexplained episode: efficient, devoted, respectful, and respectable. She was dependent on them and felt at home with them, and she evidently preferred to put the whole matter out of her mind, as far as she could. She was absolutely certain that something strange had happened in her house, and I was more than ever convinced that she had received a shock which the accident of a broken ankle was not sufficient to account for; but in the end I agreed that nothing was to be gained by cross-questioning the servants or the new doctor.

I was at Whitegates off and on that winter and during the following summer, and when I went home to New York for good early in October, I left my cousin in her old health and spirits. Dr. Selgrove had been ordered to Switzerland for the summer, and this further postponement of his return to his practice seemed to have put the happenings of the strange weekend out of her mind. Her life was going on as peacefully and normally as usual, and I left her without anxiety, and indeed without a thought of the mystery, which was now nearly a year old.

I was living then in a small flat in New York by myself, and I had hardly settled into it when, very late one evening—on the last day of October—I heard my bell ring. As it was my maid's evening out, and I was alone, I went to the door myself, and on the threshold, to my amazement, I saw Sara Clayburn. She was wrapped in a fur cloak, with a hat drawn over her forehead, and a face so pale and haggard that I saw something dreadful must have happened to her. "Sara," I gasped, not knowing what I was saying, "where in the world have you come from at this hour?"

"From Whitegates. I missed the last train and came by car." She came in and sat down on the bench near the door. I saw that she could hardly stand, and sat down beside her, putting my arm about her. "For heaven's sake, tell me what's happened."

She looked at me without seeming to see me. "I telephoned to Nixon's and hired a car. It took me five hours and a quarter to get here." She looked about her. "Can you take me in for the night? I've left my luggage downstairs."

"For as many nights as you like. But you look so ill—"

She shook her head. "No; I'm not ill. I'm only frightened—deathly frightened," she repeated in a whisper.

Her voice was so strange, and the hands I was pressing between mine were so cold, that I drew her to her

feet and led her straight to my little guest room. My
flat was in an old-fashioned building, not many stories
high, and I was on more human terms with the staff
than is possible in one of the modern Babels. I telephoned down to have my cousin's bags brought up, and
meanwhile I filled a hot water bottle, warmed the bed,
and got her into it as quickly as I could. I had never
seen her as unquestioning and submissive, and that
alarmed me even more than her pallor. She was not
the woman to let herself be undressed and put to bed
like a baby; but she submitted without a word, as though
aware that she had reached the end of her tether.

"It's good to be here," she said in a quieter tone, as
I tucked her up and smoothed the pillows. "Don't leave
me yet, will you—not just yet."

"I'm not going to leave you for more than a minute—
just to get you a cup of tea," I reassured her; and she
lay still. I left the door open, so that she could hear me
stirring about in the little pantry across the passage,
and when I brought her the tea she swallowed it grate-
fully, and a little color came into her face. I sat with
her in silence for some time; but at last she began: "You
see it's exactly a year—"

I should have preferred to have her put off till the
next morning whatever she had to tell me; but I saw
from her burning eyes that she was determined to rid
her mind of what was burdening it, and that until she
had done so it would be useless to proffer the sleeping
draft I had ready.

"A year since what?" I asked stupidly, not yet as-
sociating her precipitate arrival with the mysterious
occurrences of the previous year at Whitegates.

She looked at me in surprise. "A year since I met
that woman. Don't you remember—the strange woman
who was coming up the drive the afternoon when I
broke my ankle? I didn't think of it at the time, but it
was on All Souls' eve that I met her."

Yes, I said, I remembered that it was.

"Well—and this is All Souls' eve, isn't it? I'm not as
good as you are on Church dates, but I thought it was."

"Yes. This is All Souls' eve."

"I thought so.... Well, this afternoon I went out for
my usual walk. I'd been writing letters, and paying

bills, and didn't start till late; not till it was nearly dusk. But it was a lovely clear evening. And as I got near the gate, there was the woman coming in—the same woman...going toward the house...."

I pressed my cousin's hand, which was hot and feverish now. "If it was dusk, could you be perfectly sure it was the same woman?" I asked.

"Oh, perfectly sure, the evening was so clear. I knew her and she knew me; and I could see she was angry at meeting her. I stopped her and asked: 'Where are you going?' just as I had asked her last year. And she said, in the same queer half-foreign voice: 'Only to see one of the girls,' as she had said before. Then I felt angry all of a sudden, and I said: 'You shan't set foot in my house again. Do you hear me? I order you to leave.' And she laughed; yes, she laughed—very low, but distinctly. By that time it had got quite dark, as if a sudden storm was sweeping up over the sky, so that though she was so near me I could hardly see her. We were standing by the clump of hemlocks at the turn of the drive, and as I went up to her, furious at her impertinence, she passed behind the hemlocks, and when I followed her she wasn't there....No; I swear to you she wasn't there....And in the darkness I hurried back to the house, afraid that she would slip by me and get there first. And the queer thing was that as I reached the door the black cloud vanished, and there was the transparent twilight again. In the house everything seemed as usual, and the servants were busy about their work; but I couldn't get it out of my head that the woman, under the shadow of that cloud, had somehow got there before me." She paused for breath, and began again. "In the hall I stopped at the telephone and rang up Nixon, and told him to send a car at once to go to New York, with a man he knew to drive me. And Nixon came with the car himself...."

Her head sank back on the pillow and she looked at me like a frightened child. "It was good of Nixon," she said.

"Yes; it was very good of him. But when they saw you leaving—the servants, I mean..."

"Yes. Well, when I got upstairs to my room I rang for Agnes. She came, looking just as cool and quiet as usual. And when I told her I was starting for New York in half an hour—I said it was on account of a sudden business call—well, then her presence of mind failed her for the first time. She forgot to look surprised, she even forgot to make an objection—and you know what an objector Agnes is. And as I watched her I could see a little secret spark of relief in her eyes, though she was so on her guard. And she just said: 'Very well, madam,' and asked me what I wanted to take with me. Just as if I were in the habit of dashing off to New York after dark on an autumn night to meet a business engagement! No, she made a mistake not to show any surprise—and not even to ask me why I didn't take my own car. And her losing her head in that way frightened me more than anything else. For I saw she was so thankful I was going that she hardly dared speak, for fear she should betray herself, or I should change my mind!"

After that Mrs. Clayburn lay a long while silent, breathing less unrestfully; and at last she closed her eyes, as though she felt more at ease now that she had spoken, and wanted to sleep. As I got up quietly to leave her, she turned her head a little and murmured: "I shall never go back to Whitegates again." Then she shut her eyes and I saw that she was falling asleep.

I have set down above, I hope without omitting anything essential, the record of my cousin's strange experience as she told it to me. Of what happened at Whitegates, that is all I can personally vouch for. The rest—and of course there is a rest—is pure conjecture; and I give it only as such.

My cousin's maid, Agnes, was from the isle of Skye; and the Hebrides, as everyone knows, are full of the supernatural—whether in the shape of ghostly presences, or the almost ghostlier sense of unseen watchers peopling the long nights of those stormy solitudes. My cousin, at any rate, always regarded Agnes as the—perhaps unconscious, at any rate irresponsible—channel through which communications from the other side of the veil reached the submissive household at Whitegates. Though Agnes had been with Mrs. Clayburn for a long time without any peculiar incident revealing this affinity with the unknown forces, the power to communicate with them may all the while have been latent in the woman, only awaiting a kindred touch; and that touch may have been given by the unknown visitor whom my cousin, two years in succession, had met coming up the drive at Whitegates on the eve of All Souls'. Certainly the date bears out my hypothesis; for I suppose that, even in this unimaginative age, a few people still remember that All Souls' eve is the night when the dead can walk—and when, by the same token, other spirits, piteous or malevolent, are also freed from the restrictions which secure the earth to the living on the other days of the year.

If the recurrence of this date is more than a coincidence—and for my part I think it is—then I take it that the strange woman who twice came up the drive at Whitegates on All Souls' eve was either a "fetch," or else, more probably, and more alarmingly, a living woman inhabited by a witch. The history of witchcraft, as is well known, abounds in such cases, and such a messenger might well have been delegated by the powers who rule in these matters to summon Agnes and her fellow servants to a midnight "coven" in some neighboring solitude. To learn what happens at covens, and the reason of the irresistible fascination they exercise over the timorous and superstitious, one need only address oneself to the immense body of literature dealing with these mysterious rites. Anyone who has once felt the faintest curiosity to assist at a coven apparently soon finds the curiosity increase to desire, the desire to an uncontrollable longing, which, when the opportunity presents itself, breaks down all inhibitions; for those who have once taken part in a coven will move heaven and earth to take part again.

Such is my—conjectural—explanation of the strange happenings at Whitegates. My cousin always said she could not believe that incidents which might fit into the desolate landscape of the Hebrides could occur in the cheerful and populous Connecticut Valley; but if she did not believe, she at least feared—such moral paradoxes are not uncommon—and though she insisted that there must be some natural explanation of the mystery, she never returned to investigate it.

"No, no," she said with a little shiver, whenever I touched on the subject of her going back to Whitegates, "I don't want ever to risk seeing that woman again...." And she never went back.

YESTERDAY'S WITCH

by Gahan Wilson

Gahan Wilson (1930–   ) was born in Evanston, Illinois, and studied at the Art Institute of Chicago, graduating in 1952. His weird cartoons have appeared in many magazines, most notably Playboy, *and have been collected into numerous volumes. The same taste for the fantastic is evident in Wilson's short stories.*

A member of the Cartoonists Guild, Science Fiction Writers of America, and the Mystery Writers of America, he was instrumental in the formation of the first World Fantasy Convention, held in 1975.

Her house is gone now. Someone tore it down and bull-dozed away her trees and set up an ugly apartment building made of cheap bricks and cracking concrete on the flattened place they'd built. I drove by there a few nights ago; I'd come back to town for the first time in years to give a lecture at the university, and I saw blue TV flickers glowing in the building's living rooms.

Her house sat on a small rise, I remember, with a wide stretch of scraggly lawn between it and the iron-work fence which walled off her property from the side-walk and the rest of the outside world. The windows of her house peered down at you through a thick tangle of oak tree branches, and I can remember walking by and knowing she was peering out at me and hunching up my shoulders. Because I couldn't help it, but never, ever, giving her the satisfaction of seeing me hurry because of fear.

To the adults she was Miss Marble, but we children knew better. We knew she had another name, though none of us knew just what it was, and we knew she was a witch. I don't know who it was told me first about Miss Marble's being a witch; it might have been Billy

Drew. I think it was, but I had already guessed in spite of being less than six. I grew up, all of us grew up, sure and certain of Miss Marble's being a witch.

You never managed to get a clear view of Miss Marble, or I don't ever remember doing so, except that once. You just got peeks and hints. A quick glimpse of her wide, short body as she scuttled up the front porch steps; a brief hint of her brown-wrapped form behind a thick clump of bushes by the garage where, it was said, an electric runabout sat rusting away; a sudden flash of her fantastically wrinkled face in the narrowing slot of a closing door, and that was all.

Fred Pulley claimed he had gotten a good long look at her one afternoon. She had been weeding, or something, absorbed at digging in the ground, and off guard and careless even though she stood a mere few feet from the fence. Fred had fought down his impulse to keep on going by, and he had stood and studied her for as much as two or three minutes before she looked up and saw him and snarled and turned away.

We never tired of asking Fred about what he had seen.

"Her teeth, Fred," one of us would whisper—you almost always talked about Miss Marble in whispers—"did you see her *teeth?*"

"They're long and yellow," Fred would say. "And they come to points at the ends. And I think I saw blood on them."

None of us really believed Fred had seen Miss Marble, understand, and we certainly didn't believe that part about the blood, but we were so very curious about her, and when you're really curious about something, especially if you're a bunch of kids, you want to get all the information on the subject even if you're sure it's lies.

So we didn't believe what Fred Pulley said about Miss Marble's having blood on her teeth, nor about the bones he'd seen her pulling out of the ground, but we remembered it all the same, just in case, and it entered into any calculations we made about Miss Marble.

Halloween was the time she figured most prominently in our thoughts. First because she was a witch, of course, and second because of a time-honored ritual among the neighborhood children concerning her and ourselves and that evening of the year. It was a kind of test by fire that every male child had to go through when he reached the age of thirteen, or to be shamed forever after. I have no idea when it originated; I only know that when I attained my thirteenth year and was thereby qualified and doomed for the ordeal, the rite was established beyond question.

I can remember putting on my costume for that memorable Halloween, an old Prince Albert coat and a papier-maché mask which bore a satisfying likeness to a decayed cadaver, with the feeling I was girding myself for a great battle. I studied my reflection in a mirror affixed by swivels to my bedroom bureau and wondered gravely if I would be able to meet the challenge this night would bring. Unsure, but determined, I picked up my brown paper shopping bag, which was very large so as to accommodate as much candy as possible, said good-bye to my mother and father and dog, and went out. I had not gone a block before I met George Watson and Billy Drew.

"Have you got anything yet?" asked Billy.

"No." I indicated the emptiness of my bag. "I just started."

"The same with us," said George. And then he looked at me carefully. "Are you ready?"

"Yes," I said, realizing I had not been ready until that very moment, and feeling an encouraging glow at knowing I was. "I can do it all right."

Mary Taylor and her little sister Betty came up, and so did Eddy Baker and Phil Myers and the Arthur brothers. I couldn't see where they all had come from, but it seemed as if every kid in the neighborhood was suddenly there, crowding around under the streetlamp, costumes flapping in the wind, holding bags and boxes and staring at me with glistening, curious eyes.

"Do you want to do it now," asked George, "or do you want to wait?"

George had done it the year before and he had waited.

"I'll do it now," I said.

I began walking along the sidewalk, the others following after me. We crossed Garfield Street and Peabody Street and that brought us to Baline Avenue where we turned left. I could see Miss Marble's iron fence half a block ahead, but I was careful not to slow my pace. When we arrived at the fence I walked to the gate with as firm a tread as I could muster and put my hand upon its latch. The metal was cold and made me think of coffin handles and graveyard diggers' picks. I pushed it down and the gate swung open with a low, rusty groaning.

Now it was up to me alone. I was face to face with the ordeal. The basic terms of it were simple enough: walk down the crumbling path which led through the tall, dry grass to Miss Marble's porch, cross the porch, ring Miss Marble's bell, and escape. I had seen George Watson do it last year and I had seen other brave souls do it before him. I knew it was not an impossible task.

It was a chilly night with a strong, persistent wind and clouds scudding overhead. The moon was three-fourths full and it looked remarkably round and solid in the sky. I became suddenly aware, for the first time in my life, that it was a real *thing* up there. I wondered how many Halloweens it had looked down on and what it had seen.

I pulled the lapels of my Prince Albert coat close about me and started walking down Miss Marble's path. I walked because all the others had run or skulked, and I was resolved to bring new dignity to the test if I possibly could.

From afar the house looked bleak and abandoned, a thing of cold blues and grays and greens, but as I drew nearer, a peculiar phenomenon began to assert itself. The windows, which from the sidewalk had seemed only to reflect the moon's glisten, now began to take on a warmer glow; the walls and porch, which had seemed all shriveled, peeling paint and leprous patches of rotting wood now began to appear well-kept. I swallowed and strained my eyes. I had been prepared for a growing feeling of menace, for ever darker shadows, and this increasing evidence of warmth and tidiness absolutely baffled me.

By the time I reached the porch steps the place had taken on a positively cozy feel. I now saw that the building was in excellent repair and that it was well-painted with a smooth coat of reassuring cream. The light from the windows was now unmistakably cheerful, a ruddy, friendly pumpkin kind of orange suggesting crackling fireplaces all set and ready for toasting marshmallows. There was a very unwitchlike clump of Indian corn fixed to the front door, and I was almost certain I detected an odor of sugar and cinnamon wafting into the cold night air.

I stepped onto the porch, gaping. I had anticipated many awful possibilities during this past year. Never far from my mind had been the horrible pet Miss Marble was said to own, a something-or-other, which was all claws and scales and flew on wings with transparent webbing. Perhaps, I had thought, this thing would swoop down from the bare oak limbs and carry me off while my friends on the sidewalk screamed and screamed. Again, I had not dismissed the notion Miss Marble might turn me into a frog with a little motion of her fingers and then step on me with her foot and squish me.

But here I was feeling foolish, very young, crossing this friendly porch and smelling—I was sure of it now—sugar and cinnamon and cider and, what's more, butterscotch on top of that. I raised my hand to ring the bell and was astonished at myself for not being the least bit afraid when the door softly opened and there stood Miss Marble herself.

I looked at her and she smiled at me. She was short and plump, and she wore an apron with a thick ruffle all along its edges, and her face was smooth and red and shiny as an autumn apple. She wore bifocals on the tip of her tiny nose and she had her white hair fixed in a perfectly round bun in the exact center of the top of her head. Delicious odors wafted round her through the open door and I peered greedily past her.

"Well," she said in a mild, old voice, "I am so glad that someone has at last come to have a treat. I've waited so many years, and each year I've been ready, but nobody's come."

She stood to one side and I could see a table in the hall piled with candy and nuts and bowls of fruit and platesful of pies and muffins and cake, all of it shining and glittering in the warm, golden glow which seemed everywhere. I heard Miss Marble chuckle warmly.

"Why don't you call your friends in? I'm sure there will be plenty for all."

I turned and looked down the path and saw them, huddled in the moonlight by the gate, hunched wide-eyed over their boxes and bags. I felt a sort of generous pity for them. I walked to the steps and waved.

"Come on! It's all right!"

They would not budge.

"May I show them something?"

She nodded yes and I went into the house and got an enormous orange-frosted cake with numbers of golden sugar pumpkins on its sides.

"Look," I cried, lifting the cake into the moonlight, "Look at this! And she's got lots more! She always had, but we never asked for it!"

George was the first through the gate, as I knew he would be. Billy came next, and then Eddy, then the rest. They came slowly, at first, timid as mice, but then the smells of chocolate and tangerines and brown sugar got to their noses and they came faster. By the time they had arrived at the porch they had lost their fear, the same as I, but their astonished faces showed me how I must have looked to Miss Marble when she'd opened the door.

"Come in, children. I'm so glad you've all come at last!"

None of us had ever seen such candy or dared to dream of such cookies and cakes. We circled the table in the hall, awed by its contents, clutching at our bags.

"Take all you want, children. It's all for you."

Little Betty was the first to reach out. She got a gumdrop as big as a plum and was about to pop it into her mouth when Miss Marble said:

"Oh, no, dear, don't eat it now. That's not the way you do with tricks or treats. You wait till you get out on the sidewalk and then you go ahead and gobble it up. Just put it in your bag for now, sweetie."

Betty was not all that pleased with the idea of putting off eating her gumdrop, but she did as Miss Marble asked and plopped it into her bag and quickly followed it with other items such as licorice cats and apples dipped in caramel and pecans lumped together with some lovely-looking brown stuff and soon all the other children, myself very much included, were doing the same, filling our bags and boxes industriously, giving the task of clearing the table as rapidly as possible our entire attention.

Soon, amazingly soon, we had done it. True, there was the occasional peanut, now and then a largish crumb survived, but by and large, the job was done. What was left was fit only for rats and roaches, I thought, and then was puzzled by the thought. Where had such an unpleasant idea come from?

How our bags bulged! How they strained to hold what we had stuffed into them! How wonderfully heavy they were to hold!

Miss Marble was at the door now, holding it open and smiling at us.

"You must come back next year, sweeties, and I will give you more of the same."

We trooped out, some of us giving the table one last glance just to make sure, and then we headed down the path, Miss Marble waving us good-bye. The long, dead grass at the sides of the path brushed stiffly against our bags, making strange hissing sounds. I felt as cold as if I had been standing in the chill night air all along, and not comforted by the cozy warmth inside Miss Marble's house. The moon was higher now and seemed—I didn't know how or why—to be mocking us.

I heard Mary Taylor scolding her little sister: "She said not to eat any till we got to the sidewalk!"

"I don't care. I want some!"

The wind had gotten stronger and I could hear the stiff tree branches growl high over our heads. The fence seemed far away and I wondered why it was taking us so long to get to it. I looked back at the house and my mouth went dry when I saw that it was gray and old and dark, once more, and that the only light from its windows was reflections of the pale moon.

Suddenly little Betty Taylor began to cry, first in small, choking sobs, and then in loud wails. George Watson said: "What's wrong?" and then there was a pause, and then George cursed and threw Betty's bag over the lawn toward the house and his own box after it. They landed with a queer rustling slither that made the small hairs on the back of my neck stand up. I let go of my own bag and it flopped, bulging, into the grass by my feet. It looked like a huge, pale toad with a gaping, grinning mouth.

One by one the others rid themselves of what they carried. Some of the younger ones, whimpering, would not let go, but the older children gently separated them from the things they clutched.

I opened the gate and held it while the rest filed out onto the sidewalk. I followed them and closed the gate firmly. We stood and looked into the darkness beyond the fence. Here and there one of our abandoned boxes or bags seemed to glimmer faintly, some of them moved—I'll swear it—though others claimed it was just an illusion produced by the waving grass. All of us heard the high, thin laughter of the witch.

VICTIM OF THE YEAR

by Robert F. Young

Robert Franklin Young (1915–) is known for his polished, readable stories, which have appeared in many publications, from the Saturday Evening Post *to science fiction magazines. Ranging from the satiric to the sentimental to the allegorical, many of them are collected in two anthologies,* The Worlds of Robert F. Young *(1965) and* A Glass of Stars *(1968).*

Harold Knowles had been seeing the small brunette every Monday morning for the past six months, but their trysts were of an official rather than a romantic nature, and up until the Monday morning when he signed for his final unemployment-insurance check he had considered her no more noteworthy than the other are-you-ready-willing-and-able-to-work-sign-here-please girls who shared her duties with her behind the claimants' counter. True, he had wondered once or twice why she would never meet his gaze and on several occasions he had been mildly, if perversely, tempted to reach across the counter and tweak the wispy bangs that curled along her forehead; but up until the moment when she slipped the note into his claimant's folder, that was about as far as either his curiosity or his interest had taken him.

Immediately after performing the aforementioned act, she handed him the folder and leaned over the counter. For the first time her eyes met his, and he was astonished at their blue naiveté. "Read this as soon as you get home," she whispered. "It's important!"

Several buildings from the one that housed the employment office he stepped into a deserted store-entrance and withdrew the folder from his pocket. Pulling out the note, he unfolded it. For some time he stared

uncomprehendingly at the two frost-kissed maple leaves
it enclosed, then he transferred his attention to the
message itself. It was written in a large, almost child-
like, scrawl, but the character of its penmanship was
by far its least remarkable quality.

> Dear Harold: Tonight is Halloween and soon you
> will be in grave danger. I am a witch and I know
> about such things. As proof of my powers I am
> enclosing two magic leaves which will when you
> need them turn into $20 bills. As additional proof,
> I will make a prophecy. Your interview at Ack-
> man Innovators, Inc. this afternoon will turn out
> the same way all your other interviews have
> turned out ever since you lost your job eight months
> ago: you will not get to first base. Meet me at five
> o'clock when I get through work and I will explain
> everything.
>
> Gloria Maples

He read the message again, momentarily expecting
the words to realign themselves into sentences that
made sense. They did nothing of the sort. Girls had
written him silly notes before, but this one topped them
all.

He shook his head in an attempt to clear his thoughts.
Granted, tonight was Halloween, and granted, Halloween was supposedly the time of year when witches crept
out of their cobwebbed closets and did barrel rolls on
brooms, and granted, his run of bad luck had reached
a point where he half believed that it was attributable
to other than natural causes. But still and all!

Gradually the world reassumed its sane and sensible
aspect. The are-you-ready-willing-and-able-to-work-
sign-here-please girl was putting on a witch-act in a
naive attempt to attract his attention—that was all.
Certainly, working as she did, less than an arm's length
away from the job-placement section, she could have
found out about his forthcoming interview with Mr.
Ackman easily enough. And as for her magic leaves—

He laughed and started to throw them away. But for
some reason he changed his mind and slipped them into
his pocket instead. He wadded up the note and tossed

it into a nearby refuse can; then, putting the incident from his mind, he returned to his rooming house to get ready for his luncheon date with his girl friend, Priscilla Sturgis.

Old Mother Hubbard was in her kitchen, rattling pots and pans, when he tiptoed into the downstairs hall—he had taken to tiptoeing lately because of the twenty dollars back-rent he owed her—and as she never closed her door except at night or when she went out, he glimpsed her as he passed it. She was standing tall and almost scarecrow-thin in front of the kitchen stove, still stubbornly wearing black in deference to the husband who had been dead now for nearly ten years. Her real name was Mrs. Pasquale, and she kept a cat instead of a dog; but one of her first roomers, inspired no doubt by the hunger that sometimes shone in her dark and liquid eyes, had started the sobriquet rolling, and she had been known as "Old Mother Hubbard" ever since.

His room still smelled of the canned chicken soup he had heated for breakfast that morning, and he opened the window to air the place out. After shaving in the second-floor bathroom he combed his hair in his dresser mirror, then returned to the street. There, he lit the first of the three cigarettes he allowed himself each day and blew smoke into the October wind. On the stoop next door a little boy was industriously carving a grotesque mouth in a big pumpkin.

The site for the luncheon date was a swank restaurant across the street from the department store where Priscilla held down the job of buyer. She was already there when Harold arrived, and he joined her at her table, afflicted with that curious combination of admiration, adoration and awe which the sight of her invariably evoked in him. She was sunlight and laughter made woman. Her eyes were as golden as October days and her hair was the hue of Indian maize; her smile was Indian summer. Small wonder that, in a vain attempt to augment his savings and thereby expedite their wedding date, he had exchanged his suburban apartment in Forestview for a cheap room in the city; small wonder that his bitterness over the misfortunes that had dogged his footsteps ever since should be all the more acute.

But you'd never have known from the warmth of her smile that in the space of eight months he had been reduced from a prosperous suburbanite to a near-penniless city dweller with nothing between him and starvation but a five-dollar bill and a final unemployment-insurance check. "Hi, doll," she said. "Coming to my party tonight?"

"I—I don't know," he said, thinking of the outdated cut of his best suit and wondering, as he had the first time she'd asked him, why she hadn't made it a masquerade party in honor of the occasion.

"Oh, but you've just got to come, Harold! We're going to bob for apples and pin the tail on the donkey and dance and everything. Not only that, Uncle Vic is going to be there, and he's just dying to meet you!"

She was originally from out of town, and Uncle Vic, so far as Harold had ever been able to ascertain, was her only living relative. "All right," he agreed reluctantly. "What time does it begin?"

"Seven-thirty—and don't you dare show up a second later. Wait'll you see the Halloween cake I baked—it's out of this world!"

She only had an hour for lunch, and it flew by. Over their second coffees she told him about the palatial new elementary school with the two swimming pools which the Forestview citizens had voted to build and about how the school tax would double itself within five years as a consequence. He was not surprised: as a one-time denizen of the community he knew full well how the citizens doted on their offspring. Almost before he knew it, it was time to pay the check, and after signaling the waitress, he reached into his pocket and pulled out what he thought was the lonely five-dollar bill. It was so crisp and new that it crackled between his fingers, and that was odd because when he had put it into his pocket it had been old and crinkled. Looking at it, he discovered that it had changed in other ways too: it had Andrew Jackson's picture on it instead of Abraham Lincoln's, and in each of its corners the numeral 20 stood out bold and clear.

An icy wind blew down the back of his neck and set

his nerve ends to tingling. Hurriedly he pulled out the pocket's remaining contents. They consisted of two articles: another crisp twenty, and the missing five.

He became aware that he was the focal point of two pairs of eyes. One pair—Priscilla's—were a lambent gold. The other pair—the waitress's—were an impatient hazel. Hastily he paid the check with one of the twenties, and after receiving his change, escorted Priscilla across the street to the department store. She looked at him curiously when they reached the entrance and he thought for a moment that she was going to question him about his sudden wealth. But she didn't. All she said was, "See you tonight, doll—'bye."

His interview was scheduled for three o'clock. He killed the lion's share of the intervening two hours on a bench in the park, examining the pros and cons of the reality of witches. He arrived at the following conclusions: (1) in common with alchemy, witchcraft was a product of the Dark Ages and held up not one whit better in the uncompromising light of modern science; (2) there was a logical explanation behind the seemingly miraculous metamorphosis of the maple leaves (he didn't know what it was but he was darned if he was going to lose faith in the scientific light because of a dark corner or two); and (3) the are-you-ready-willing-and-able-to-work-sign-here-please girl knew about as much about sorcery as she probably knew about sex.

Feeling better, he left the park and took a bus to Ackman Innovators, Inc. The girl behind the receptionist's desk looked at him with hostile brown eyes when he handed her the card which he had received in the morning's mail from the job-placement division. She glanced at it, then promptly handed it back. "Mr. Ackman isn't in right now," she said coldly. "However, if he'd had an appointment to interview you I'm sure he would have told me."

Harold was dumbfounded. "But—"

"And anyway," the girl continued, "we're not doing any hiring at the moment. Come back in about two months."

Two months! "But this card says—"

"Two months," the girl repeated firmly. "Good day, sir."

It was a grim young man who stepped into the street a moment later and headed for the bus stop, and it was a grim young man who got off the bus some ten minutes later and made a beeline for the employment-office. The girl on duty behind the job-placement counter proved to be as much in the dark as he was. "Why don't you go back tomorrow?" she suggested. "In the meantime I'll—"

"Not in a million years!" he said. Turning to leave, he saw the are-you-ready-willing-and-able-to-work-sign-here-please girl who had slipped the note into his folder regarding him earnestly from behind the claimants' counter, and for the second time that day an icy wind blew down the back of his neck. He remembered her name: Gloria Maples. *Gloria Maples*, he said to himself grimly, descending the stairs to the street. *Avocation— Witch.*

His new wealth rendered further adherence to his poverty-induced cigarette schedule unnecessary, so he bought a pack of filter tips in a nearby drugstore; then he returned to the employment-office building and waited by the doorway till five o'clock came. He was halfway through his fourth cigarette when she finally stepped into the street.

Her blue eyes brightened when she saw him. "Hi," she said. "We'll go to my apartment—I can talk better there."

She lived in a third-floor walk-up in a rooming house almost as run-down as Old Mother Hubbard's. He followed her through a small kitchen into a slightly larger living room. It contained a battered mohair sofa, a battered mohair chair and a wobbly glass-topped coffee table. There was a three-legged black cat, with part of its tail missing, sleeping on the sofa.

Gloria sat down beside it, picked it up and placed it gently on her lap. "Matilda, this is Harold," she said. "Harold, this is my cat, Matilda."

Harold took the mohair chair. "What happened to her other leg?"

"She got run over by a hit-and-run driver and I found

her lying in the street and took her to a vet. He—he wanted to put her away but I wouldn't let him. Nobody ever claimed her so I kept her. A—a witch is supposed to have a black cat."

He looked at her contemplatively. Half an hour ago he had firmly believed her to be a witch; now the mere idea of such a thing seemed utterly preposterous. Why, she was as naive as a May morning! Naive or not, however, she still had some explaining to do. He fixed her with uncompromising eyes. "Please to begin," he said.

"I—I will." She stroked Matilda's back with nervous fingertips. "I'll—I'll begin at the beginning. First of all, I'm not a full-fledged witch yet—I'm an apprentice witch. You see, the coven sisters in the various districts are always on the lookout for potential witches, and whenever they hear of someone who's discontented and bitter they contact her through their underlings and offer to send her through witch school. It's only a one-year course, but they're awfully strict, and if you're caught doing something a respectable witch wouldn't do, you're disqualified. For—for instance, if the coven sister who nominated you our class guinea pig ever finds out I'm trying to help you she'll have me expelled immediately—and—and not only that, she may try to do me in too."

Harold lit a cigarette. He took a deep drag. "What?" he asked a little desperately, "is a class guinea pig?"

"I—I was coming to that," Gloria said. "You see, each Candlemas the senior coven sister of the three local covens nominates a Victim of the Year and turns him over to the apprentice-witch class till Allhallows Eve for them to practice their sorcery on. Then, on Allhallows Eve, she takes over and tries to do him in in some diabolical way. This—this year you were nominated.

"My—my classmates and I vied with each other in doing mean things to you. First we fixed it so you'd get laid off, and then we caused your ex-employer to tell the employment-office that you quit so you'd have to wait six weeks for your first unemployment-insurance check and wouldn't have enough money to keep up your payments on your car and would lose it, and ever since then we've been conjuring up antagonism toward you in the minds of the other local employers and their office personnel, and—and all the while I kept seeing you come in every week to sign for your checks and saw how frayed your sleeves were getting and—and how sad you were and—and— Do—do you remember that quart of milk you brought home one time and it turned out to be sour when—when you got around to drinking it? Well, I'm the one that soured it, and oh, Harold, I'm so ashamed of myself I could just lie right down and die!" And before his startled eyes she burst into tears and ran out into the kitchen.

Matilda had alighted on all three feet, and now she came over and began rubbing her furry sides against his pant leg. He patted her head abstractedly, shaken in spite of himself. He *had* been laid off; his ex-employer *had* told the employment-insurance office he had quit; he *had* lost his car; —everything that Gloria had said, in short, was true.

Granted; but that didn't mean she was *responsible* for his job difficulties—it merely meant that she knew about them. And as an are-you-ready-willing-and-able-to-work-sign-here-please girl, how could she help knowing about them? As for the sour-milk incident, she could have gotten the information from Old Mother Hubbard; after all, it was the old lady's refrigerator that the milk had gone sour in.

Presently he heard her moving about in the kitchen, and in a little while she appeared in the doorway. "Come—come out and sit down, Harold," she said. "I—I fixed us some sandwiches."

The sandwiches were peanut butter. He ate three and washed them down with two glasses of milk. She ate half a one and drank half a glass of milk. Some of the milk clung to her upper lip in a moist white film. "You've no idea how much better I feel, now that I've got my wickedness off my chest," she said. "You will be careful tonight, won't you? The best thing to do is stay where there's lots of people. It's hard for a witch to hex you when you're in a crowd."

He looked at her milk mustache, growing more amused by the second. "I'm going to my girl friend's Halloween party, so I should be safe enough," he said.

She dropped her eyes. "I—I guess you'll be safe enough there, all right. It would be better, though, if you stayed somewhere where there are plenty of policemen. Witches are leery of the law. Devil's deputies, too. His—his majesty insists on outward conformity and good citizenship, and if any of his employees get caught doing something even a little bit illegal, he gives them the ax, and bingo!—their power is gone."

"You mean 'the pitchfork,' not the ax, don't you?" Harold said, holding back his laughter.

"This is no time to be facetious, Harold. Don't you realize that your very life is at stake?"

She got up and returned the bottle of milk to the refrigerator. Then she picked up the jar of peanut butter and carried it over to a tall cupboard by the sink. He gasped when she opened the door. Every one of the shelves were filled with similar jars, and in some cases they were piled two high.

"Good lord!" he said. "Is that all you ever eat?"

She faced him shyly. "Not—not exactly. I eat lunch in the cafeteria across the street from the office. I—I was never very good at cooking. Back home, Mom did it all, and when I got transferred here there was no one to teach me."

He stood up. How she had prophesied the outcome of his interview he would probably never know, but one thing he did know: she wasn't any more to blame for the way it had turned out than she was to blame for the way all the others had turned out. After she got over her complex, he would return the two twenties to her, and perhaps then she would explain how she had tricked him into believing when he had first looked at them that they were maple leaves. It would be futile to ask her now.

"Well, thank you for the sandwiches," he said.

She accompanied him to the door. Something about her forlorn aspect prompted him to give her Priscilla's telephone number. "In case you need me for anything," he explained. "And now I've got to go."

"Good—good-bye, Harold. And be very careful, please."

There were witches galore in the streets, not to mention goblins, ghosts, brownies, and spacemen; however, he was in no mood for trick-or-treaters, and he hailed the first cab that came along. For some reason he couldn't get Gloria out of his mind. He was so preoccupied with her, in fact, that when he entered the rooming house he didn't remember to tiptoe till he came opposite Old Mother Hubbard's door and saw the old lady standing before the stove, stirring the steaming contents of a large black kettle with a long wooden spoon. It was too late then, for she had already heard him. Setting the spoon aside, she came swiftly through the doorway, hunger shining in her eyes, her black cat tagging at her heels.

He remembered the second twenty just in time and thrust it into her hand when she came up to him; then he brushed past her and hurried up the stairs. In his room he donned his best suit and surveyed himself in the dresser mirror. He could get by all right, he decided—provided that he stayed in the background. The background was where he belonged anyway.

Forestview was a half hour's ride by bus, so the sooner he got started, the better. He descended the stairs, tying his tie on the way down. Old Mother Hubbard was nowhere to be seen, but the contents of her kettle were bubbling audibly and giving off a gamy odor that permeated the entire downstairs hall. He was glad when he reached the street. The sky was overcast and the air had grown appreciably cooler. Turning up his suitcoat collar, he headed for the bus stop. Thirty-five minutes later he arrived in Forestview.

Priscilla's house was a modern American-Colonial and stood at the end of a maple-bordered street. Cars jammed its driveway and were parked along the curb halfway to the corner. Many of them had out-of-state license plates; in her capacity as buyer, Priscilla traveled a lot and met many out-of-town people. She answered his ring, resplendent in a sequined sheath. "Hi, doll, come on in," she said warmly. "Everybody's just dying to meet you!"

There were almost forty people present, and Priscilla must have praised him to the skies, judging from the enthusiastic way they responded when she introduced him. Especially Uncle Vic, who turned out to be a tall wiry individual in his sixties, with crew-cut white hair, keen blue eyes, and a firm handclasp. "Come on out to the bar," he told Harold, "and I'll mix you a drink."

The "bar" was the breakfast counter. Uncle Vic made him a stiff highball. "Priscilla's quite a girl, don't you think?" he asked, handing it to him. "Wait'll you see some of the innovations she's dreamed up for a little later on in the evening!"

"Are you from around here, sir?" Harold asked, still somewhat dazed from Priscilla's resplendence.

"Oh yes. I'm district manager for Schierke and Elend Enterprises. Quite a famous international concern — though probably you've never heard of it. Let's join the others, shall we?"

Priscilla's stereo was going full blast and the living room rug had been rolled up and stashed away in a corner. Priscilla was dancing with a tall young man as darkly handsome as she was radiantly beautiful. Harold, his diffidence routed by the highball he had drunk, cut in. She was feather-light in his arms, and her eyes were golden mirrors in which he saw the world, and the world was a roseate and wondrous thing.

Uncle Vic whirled by, a dark-haired dowager in his arms. He winked at Harold broadly. The lights grew soft, warm. Time tiptoed from the room —

Suddenly the ringing of the phone stabbed through the stereo throb of the music. "Excuse me," Priscilla said, slipping from his arms and going into the hall. She appeared a moment later in the doorway, the receiver in her hand. "It's for you," she said.

He took the receiver from her and raised it to his ear. "Hello?"

"Harold?" It was Gloria's voice. "Are you all right, Harold?"

He was annoyed. "Of course I'm all right," he said gruffly. "Why shouldn't I be?"

"Be — because they found out about us — the coven sisters, I mean. Tonight when I went to witch class the head instructress told me I was through and that I'd get my comeuppance before midnight."

"Nonsense, Gloria! You've let this obsession of yours get the best of you."

"But it's not an obsession, it's real. Oh, Harold, I'm so scared!"

She was almost hysterical. Slowly his annoyance gave way before a mental picture of her sitting forlornly in her little living room, her blue eyes dark with terror. "All right," he said abruptly, "I'll come over for a while. Pull yourself together."

He hung up. Priscilla was standing in the living room doorway, looking at him oddly. "You'll have to excuse me for an hour or so," he said. "Something's come up."

"But doll, I was just going to start the games. At least stay long enough to help us pin the tail on the—the donkey."

"I'm sorry, Pris—I can't."

She came very close to him and playfully gripped his lapels. "I won't let you go unless you promise to come back."

"All right," he said. "I promise."

He took a cab, hoping to save time, but a traffic jam thwarted him and it was a full forty minutes later when he climbed the three flights of stairs to Gloria's walk-up. When she failed to answer his knock, he pushed the door open and stepped inside. He found her in the little living room, huddled on the mohair sofa, her shoulders shaking. On the floor at her feet lay her black cat, its three legs jutting grotesquely from its lifeless body.

He went over and sat down beside her and put his arms around her. Slowly her shoulders quieted. "She—she dropped dead about ten minutes ago," she said. "Oh why did they have to pick on her—*why?*"

Tears ran down her cheeks, and she pressed her face against his lapel. He saw the way it was with her now; now he understood. Young men like himself, laughing at her, treating her like a child when she wanted to be treated like a woman; buying her candy when she craved flowers. No wonder she had wanted to become a witch—and, conversely, no wonder she hadn't been able to become one. "How did they find out about us, Gloria?" he asked gently.

"The coven sister who nominated you Victim of the Year learned that you had magic money in your possession—a witch can spot it right away—and told the head instructress. The head instructress was furious. She—she lined all of us up along the wall and threatened to torture us till one of us confessed, and I didn't want to see the other girls suffer so I said I was the one. What made it worse was that I've been sneaking into the coven library when no one was there and reading forbidden books. That's how I was able to energize the chlorophyll and induce the chromatolysis effect that—"

His voice was cold. "Who is this coven sister, Gloria?"

"I—I don't know. I've never seen any of them. An apprentice witch isn't permitted in their presence. But she must be someone you're acquainted with."

He stood up. "Never mind. *I* know who she is. I have to go now, Gloria, but I promise I'll be back."

Old Mother Hubbard's door was closed. He pounded on it peremptorily. He pounded on it again. He tried the knob. It would not turn.

The gamy odor still permeated the hall. Probably, he thought bitterly, she had taken her unholy brew to the local Sabbat and was even now presiding over it with her gaunt unlovely sisters, the devil's deputy, in his woolly goat-robe, standing at her side. Well, he would wait for her to return. He would sit on the stairs and wait till she came in the door and then he would tell her straight to her face what he thought of blackhearted old women who preyed on harmless girls and murdered crippled cats.

He got out his cigarettes, felt in his pocket for his matches. The folder was empty. There was another one in his dresser drawer, he remembered, and he went upstairs to get it. Opening the drawer, he paused. On top of the dresser lay a crisp twenty-dollar bill. Beside it lay a sheet of yellow tablet paper.

Wonderingly he picked the paper up. On it, the following words had been laboriously printed with a soft-lead pencil:

Every day when I clean your room I smell the canned soup you cook each night and morning and it is heavy on my heart that one so fine should suffer. Tonight I want to say, Harold, will you share with me the spaghetti with venison meatballs that I cook all afternoon on my stove, but you will not listen and you give me money and walk away. Now I give it back. Twenty dollars I will never need so much that good food someone cannot buy. I go now to St. Anthony's to say a prayer for you.

He stood there immobile for a long time, staring at the simple words. Hunger in a person's eyes did not always imply greed; sometimes it implied a need for understanding, a need to help, a need not to be alone.

At length he left the room and descended the stairs. The hall phone rang just as he was passing it. He took down the receiver. "Hello?"

"Hello," a man's voice answered. "I'd like to speak to Mr. Knowles."

"This is Mr. Knowles."

"This is Mr. Ackman. I hope you'll forgive me for having forgotten about our appointment this afternoon. Why I did, I don't know. Anyway, I just remembered it a moment ago—out of a clear blue sky, so to speak—so if you're still interested I'd like you to drop around tomorrow morning. I'm sure I can work something out for you."

"I'll say I'm still interested!" Harold said. "And thank you for calling."

He took a cab back to Forestview. Halfway there, the plan came to him, and he had the driver stop at an all-night drugstore. After buying a cake of soap, he climbed back into the cab. During the remainder of the ride he occupied himself by figuring out the details. It was a simple plan, and there weren't very many of them; but thinking of them kept his mind off the sickness in the pit of his stomach.

After the driver let him off in front of Priscilla's he waited till the cab disappeared around the corner, then he soaped all the windshields of the cars standing in the driveway and along the curb, and removed the valves from all the tires. When he was finished he walked half a block to an all-night service station and made a phone call. Then he returned to Priscilla's.

The party was in full swing. Her eyes lit up when he walked in the door, and a few minutes later she brought in a cake from the kitchen and set it on a card table in the middle of the living room. It was a big three-layer cake with orange frosting. In its center stood two tiny wax dolls, and around them, arranged in the shape of a pentagram, were thirty-one candles. A glimmering of the truth struck him then, and he peered at the dolls intently. One of them bore a faint resemblance to him; the other bore a faint resemblance to Gloria.

Still he found it hard to believe. Not Priscilla of the golden eyes, the golden hair; not Priscilla of the golden soul. He saw the big rectangular poster hanging on the wall then, and he had to believe. It was the pin-the-tail-on-the-donkey poster, and there were scores of tiny pinpricks in the painted animal's body. Only the animal wasn't a donkey, it was a cat—a three-legged black cat with half a tail. It had a whole tail now, though—

Not that it would need one anymore.

Priscilla was lighting the candles, and everyone was standing around the card table, looking at him eagerly. Greedily. He noticed something then—something that his previous absorption with Priscilla had wiped from his awareness. The women outnumbered the men by a ratio of twelve to one.

The candle flames leaped up in little flickerings and presently, as the wax dolls began to melt, he felt the first faint prickling of the heat. Uncle Vic leaned toward him, his face thinner somehow, his nose more pointed. Priscilla, her task completed, leaned toward him also. Her face was thinner too, and her golden eyes had transmuted to a baleful yellow. Her lips were drawn back, revealing preternaturally pointed eyeteeth. It was a masquerade party after all, and the time for unmasking had come. He shuddered at the realization.

"But why, Priscilla?" he asked, fighting to control his horror. *"Why?"*

The yellow eyes incandesced. "You love me don't you? Well, I'm returning your love in the only way I can. I'm returning it with hate—and I'm returning it in full measure!"

He drew back. The candle flames grew brighter, warmer. The first drops of sweat dampened his forehead. He held himself tight, listening with all his being. At last he heard the sound he was waiting for—the slamming of a car door. He relaxed then.

"What was that?" Uncle Vic asked sharply.

"The police, I imagine," Harold said. "I asked them to drop by."

"It can't be," Priscilla said shrilly. "Why, if you even mentioned the word *Sabbat* they'd laugh at you!"

"I kind of thought they would—that's why I didn't mention it. I asked them to drop by for quite another reason. Wait'll you see what the kids have done to your cars."

She was staring at him. So was Uncle Vic. So were the others. "Our cars—" she began. Then, "Oh, you mean they soaped the windows and things like that." She laughed. "We'll simply refuse to prefer charges—won't we, Uncle Vic?"

Uncle Vic relaxed visibly. "Sure, that's what we'll do."

"Who," Harold said, wiping his forehead, "said anything about you preferring charges?" He confronted Priscilla. "Obviously you aren't familiar with Forestview's ordinances. The one I have in mind states that on the night of October thirty-first all private vehicles shall be kept in garages, either public or private, in order that 'our citizens of tomorrow will not be tempted to perform acts of a delinquent nature.' The local kids have been behaving so well for the past several years that the ordinance has been unofficially laid to rest, but I imagine that once the chief of police hears about your flagrant violation of it he'll be delighted to revive it."

Abruptly Uncle Vic blew out the candles. "You fool!" he said to Priscilla. "You utter fool!" His voice rose. "The old man will be furious. He'll strip us of our powers—every one of us. I'll lose my vicariate! Why didn't you check on the ordinances? Why didn't—"

"Shut up, you old goat!" Priscilla screamed. "He's lying, don't you see? The police aren't out there! There's no one out there! He's lying, I tell you. He's—"

The doorbell rang.

It was nearing midnight when Harold got back to the city. But late though the hour was, there was still time to go trick-or-treating. First he would pick up Gloria, he decided, and then the two of them would go calling on Mrs. Pasquale. And if the old lady didn't come across with two plates of her spaghetti with venison meatballs, they would soap her windows but good.

COLLECTIONS OF TALES FROM THE MASTERS OF MYSTERY, HORROR AND SUSPENSE

Edited by Carol-Lynn Rössel Waugh, Martin Harry Greenberg and Isaac Asimov

Each volume contains an introduction by Isaac Asimov.

Thirteen Horrors of Halloween is a devil's dozen of ghoulish delights, filled with bewitching tales of murder and the macabre by such celebrated authors as Isaac Asimov, Ray Bradbury, Edward D. Hoch, Ellery Queen and Edith Wharton.
84814-7/$2.95

The Big Apple Mysteries is an anthology of 13 detective stories set in the vibrant, electric—and sometimes dangerous—city of New York, written by such super authors as Rex Stout, Edward D. Hoch and Stuart Palmer.
80150-7/$2.75

The Twelve Crimes of Christmas
When twelve masters, including Dorothy L. Sayers, Robert Somerlott and Ellery Queen, get into the holiday spirit, it's time to trim the tree, deck the halls...and bury the bodies. Here are a dozen baffling tales of murder and mischief committed during the so-called merry season.
78931-0/$2.50

AVON Paperbacks